IT WAS A VERY BAD YEAR

The Rat Pack Mysteries from Robert J Randisi

EVERYBODY KILLS SOMEBODY SOMETIME
LUCK BE A LADY, DON'T DIE
HEY THERE – YOU WITH THE GUN IN YOUR HAND
YOU'RE NOBODY 'TIL SOMEBODY KILLS YOU
I'M A FOOL TO KILL YOU *
FLY ME TO THE MORGUE *
IT WAS A VERY BAD YEAR *

* *available from Severn House*

IT WAS A VERY BAD YEAR

A 'Rat Pack' Mystery

Robert J. Randisi

This first world edition published 2012
in Great Britain and in the USA by
SEVERN HOUSE PUBLISHERS LTD of
9–15 High Street, Sutton, Surrey, England, SM1 1DF.

British Library Cataloguing in Publication Data

Randisi, Robert J.
It was a very bad year.
1. Sinatra, Frank, 1915-1998–Fiction. 2. Sinatra, Frank, Jr., 1944- –Fiction. 3. Gianelli, Eddie (Fictitious character)–Fiction. 4. Detective and mystery stories.
I. Title
813.6-dc23

ISBN-13: 978-0-7278-8191-5 (cased)

All Severn House titles are printed on acid-free paper.

Severn House Publishers support The Forest Stewardship Council [FSC], the leading international forest certification organisation. All our titles that are printed on Greenpeace-approved FSC-certified paper carry the FSC logo.

Typeset by Palimpsest Book Production Ltd.,
Falkirk, Stirlingshire, Scotland.
Printed and bound in Great Britain by
MPG Books Ltd., Bodmin, Cornwall.

To Marthayn,
Who makes every year a very
good year for me.

'But now the days grow short,
I'm in the autumn of the year . . .'

Lyrics by Ivor Arthur Davies

AUTHOR'S NOTE

This is a work of fiction. To the author's knowledge Miss Abby Dalton has never at any point in her life posed for risqué photos. In her career she has exhibited nothing but grace and dignity.

PROLOGUE

Las Vegas, May 12, 2006

Let me tell you about being an octogenarian.

You can't do the things you used to do, at the ripe old age of eighty. You can't eat the things you like, because now it's all bad for you. And what you *can* eat that *is* good for you is either grey or green.

The other thing is, you read the newspaper. Specifically, the obituaries. It's always a good news/bad news thing. Good when your own name isn't there, bad seeing all the familiar names.

One name that caught my attention was Floyd Patterson. At twenty-one, Patterson was the youngest heavyweight title holder in history. At seventy-one, he had succumbed to Alzheimer's disease and prostate cancer.

'What's the matter? You look like you just lost your last friend.'

I looked up at Mark Hancock. Mark held in The Venetian Resort Hotel and Casino the job I once held in the Sands. The Venetian now stood where the Sands had existed until its implosion in 1996. That was one of the reasons I liked to take my breakfast there. It wasn't the same place, but it was *in* the same place. If you get my meaning. I can't explain it, but it was a comfort to me.

Mark sat down across from me. He ran his hand over his black hair, shot through with grey. It was a habit he had acquired since turning fifty a couple of years ago. Mark had started to feel old. Maybe that's why he liked having breakfast with me.

What I wouldn't give to be fifty again.

'That's not something you want to say to someone my age, Mark,' I said.

'Oh, yeah,' he said. 'Sorry.' He signaled to the waitress for coffee, and snatched a menu from the table.

'As a matter of fact, I have lost a friend,' I said. 'Floyd Patterson died.'

'Yeah, I heard that on the news,' he said. Then: 'Wait. You knew Floyd Patterson?'

'You haven't been listening to me,' I said. 'I knew everybody.'

'Well, I know you knew everybody in the entertainment field,' Mark said. 'Frank, Dino, Sammy, and like that. But I didn't know you knew sports figures.'

'Sports isn't entertainment?' I asked.

'Well, maybe now . . .'

He was right. Back then sports – especially boxing – was not considered part of the entertainment field. Although Muhammad Ali – who I first met when he was Cassius Clay – was doing his best to change that.

Mark ordered his breakfast from the fresh-faced waitress, watched her walk away and then turned back to me.

'So did you know Mike Tyson?' he asked.

'I met him,' I said. 'I wouldn't say I knew him.'

'But you knew Floyd Patterson?'

'Very well,' I said.

'You goin' to his funeral?'

'I don't travel much these days, Mark,' I said. 'I especially don't fly.'

'Can't say I blame you for that,' he said, nodding. 'You could get trampled in an airport.'

Or a mall, I thought. Especially when your feet are numb from diabetes. No, I pretty much stayed close to home, these days.

'I hadn't seen Floyd in a long time,' I explained. 'We lost touch. I'm sorry he died the way he did, and too soon.'

To somebody my age, seventy-one was too soon.

Mark's bacon-and-eggs breakfast came. I looked down at my bran cereal and fruit. If I ate what Mark was eating my sugar would soar sky high. Luckily, I could still drink coffee, but no more orange juice for me. I remembered the days I used to watch my buddy Jerry Epstein pack away a couple of stacks of pancakes. Now he was recovering from prostate cancer. As soon as he was well enough he said he was going to visit me. I was afraid when he got off the plane I'd see a shadow of what Jerry once was. That was certainly what he would see when he looked at me. But Jerry was in his seventies, and if he kicked the cancer he'd still be as healthy as a horse.

Floyd Patterson was beyond that, though. He was gone. In his prime he was small for a heavyweight, about a hundred-and-eighty pounds, but he was fast and strong. The only times he lost was when he came up against somebody faster, and stronger. Ingemar Johansson, Muhammad Ali, and Sonny Liston came to mind.

'Hey, didn't Patterson fight Liston in Las Vegas years ago?' Mark asked.

'He did,' I said. 'It was the rematch.'

'OK, now wait,' Mark said. 'Tell me you were there that night.'

'I was there that night,' I said.

'Really?'

'Yes, really.'

'Oh, man!' Mark said. 'What I wouldn't have given to see that fight.'

'It wasn't much of a fight, as I remember,' I said. There were other things I remembered about that night, though. And other people . . . lots of other people . . .

'That was nineteen-sixty three. I was a bigger stud then than you are now, kid . . .'

ONE

Las Vegas Convention Center, July 22, 1963

'Hang on to your hat,' Nick Conte said. 'This isn't gonna take long.'

Richard Conte – a tough-guy actor whose close friends all called him 'Nick' for the simple reason that it was his real first name – was seated to my right, Frank Sinatra to my left.

'You're crazy,' Frank said. 'That first fight was a fluke. Liston's way too slow for Floyd.'

Conte leaned forward to look past me at Frank.

'Wanna double the bet?' he asked.

'You're on, pally,' Frank said. 'Floyd takes his title back tonight.'

Nick looked at me. 'You want a piece?'

'I'm not gamblin' on this fight,' I said. 'My heart is with Floyd, but . . . I don't know. Liston looks tough.'

'See?' Nick said to Frank. 'Even Eddie says Liston wins.'

'He didn't say that,' Frank said. 'He just said Liston looks tough. Well, he ain't gonna scare Floyd to death.'

'Well, he scared him enough to KO him in two minutes the first time,' Conte said. 'I don't see it goin' too much longer than that this time.'

'You're crazy . . .' Frank said, but I didn't hear the rest.

I had to admit, Sonny Liston was sorta scaring me to death, and I wasn't even in the ring with him. The knockout in the first fight – which actually came at two minutes six seconds into the first round – had been devastating to Floyd. I wasn't sure he was fully recovered yet, psychologically. And he did look less than confident to me in the ring.

'What the hell—' I heard Frank say.

'What?' I asked, turning around.

He was looking not at the ring, but across it.

'What's that bum doin' here?' he asked.

'Who?'

'Across the ring.' He pointed. 'That fella's name is Amsler, Joe Amsler.'

I tried to see who he was pointing at.

'Which one?'

'The young guy,' Frank said, 'right across from us. He went to high school with my Nancy.'

I saw an animated young man talking earnestly with another man about the same age. It looked to me like they weren't looking at the ring either, but past it to us – at Frank.

'I take it you don't like him?'

Frank looked at me and said, 'I never like any boy who hangs around Nancy. Keep that in mind, Eddie.'

'Hey,' I said, referring to my one close encounter with Frank's daughter, 'she flirted with me.'

'Just remember, pally,' he said, poking me in the chest with his forefinger.

After that we ignored Amsler and went back to watching the action in the ring.

Richard Conte nudged me and asked, 'Would it be bad taste for me to light up a victory cigar now?'

'I don't think Floyd's camp would appreciate it.'

'OK,' he said, 'I'll hold off. Floyd may not be able to beat Liston, but he could kick my ass with no trouble.'

'You and me both,' I agreed.

We watched as the fighters came to the center of the ring for their instructions.

A left took Floyd's legs out from under him, and set up the first knockdown.

'Oops,' Conte said, happily.

Floyd got up and indicated to the ref that he was all right, but you could see he had no legs. A barrage of punches put him down for a second time, and Conte happily took out his cigar. He was just taking the cellophane off when Floyd went down for the third and final time.

He was knocked out at two minutes ten seconds of round one.

He had lasted four seconds longer than the first fight.

Liston would defend his title against Cassius Clay the following year.

Conte's blue cigar smoke surrounded us as we waited for the fight crowd to clear out.

Conte puffed away happily.

Sinatra fanned away the smoke and said, 'Gloat now, Nick, but Cassius Clay will take the title away from Liston when they meet.'

'You wanna bet now?' Conte asked, smiling.

I didn't get in on that bet, either. I didn't think anyone would be beating Sonny Liston for a long time.

By the time we left the Las Vegas Convention Center I had completely forgotten about Joe Amsler.

TWO

Las Vegas, November 1963

I first met Abby Dalton briefly when I was in LA with Ava Gardner. We flirted some, but let me repeat that at the time I was with Ava Gardner. Abby was a beautiful young blonde with a delicious overbite (although I *had* heard it described as 'vicious') who was playing Joey Bishop's wife on his sitcom *The Joey Bishop Show*.

Joey had called me the day before to say he was coming into town and did I want to have dinner? Whenever any of the guys flew in I made time for them. We agreed to meet at the Bootlegger Italian restaurant on the South Strip. Frank and Dean had introduced me to the Bootlegger, which served traditional Italian fare.

I arrived first and was sitting at a table with a martini when Joey walked in. I was surprised to see that Abby Dalton was with him. Her hair was up, and she was wearing a suit that did nothing to hide her curves, a short skirt and high heels that showed off her wonderful legs.

'Hey, Eddie,' Joey said, as they approached, 'you remember Abby.'

'How could I forget?' I asked, standing. 'Nice to see you again, Miss Dalton.'

'Oh, please, Eddie,' she said, dazzling me with that overbite, 'call me Abby.'

'All right, Abby. Please, sit.'

She looked at the two place settings on the table and turned to Joey.

'You didn't tell him I was coming.'

Joey looked at me for help.

'No, he didn't,' I said, and his look turned to a glare, 'but it's a pleasant surprise.'

'Well,' she said, 'somebody's a gentleman.'

Joey took the hint and held her chair for her. A waiter came running over – because he recognized Joey, or simply because he saw Abby? – and asked if they wanted drinks.

'I'll have a Coke,' Joey said, as he sat. According to him he had never touched hard liquor in his life, and I never saw a reason to doubt him.

'I'll have what Eddie's having,' Abby said.

'Vodka martini coming up, signorina.' I could see in the young waiter's eyes that he was smitten.

'Eddie, I'm sorry Joey surprised you like this,' Abby said.

'No reason to apologize,' I said. 'Why would I not want to eat dinner with a beautiful woman – and a schmuck?'

'Hey, easy now.' Joey looked sharp, as usual, in a black suit, white shirt and thin black tie. He always made me feel like a bargain basement kind of guy as I looked down at my own five-year-old suit.

'Well, I'm sure he got you here under false pretenses,' she said. 'You see, I have a problem that Joey said you might be able to help me with.'

There was a time when I thought Frank, Dean, Joey and the rest only called me when they had problems. That time had past, since I'd had many breakfasts and dinners with each of them that involved nothing more than catching up.

'Well, Joey's pretty well versed on what I can and can't do,' I told her. 'If he says I can help you, I probably can. At the very least, I'll try.'

'See?' Joey said to her. 'What did I tell you? He's the best.'

The waiter returned with their drinks, and a third place setting.

'We won't need that,' Joey said. 'I'll be leaving right after I finish my Coke.'

'Si, signore,' the waiter said, and took the extra setting away.

Joey looked at me. 'I just wanted to get you two started,

then I figured I'd leave you alone so Abby can tell you her troubles.'

Did this mean that Joey had promised her I'd help, even without knowing what the problem was?

'Well then,' I said, 'you should probably leave so we can order.'

Joey drank half his Coke and said, 'Oh, yeah, right.' He stood up. 'You'll see that Abby gets back to the Sands?'

'Of course I will,' I said.

Joey put his hand on her shoulder and said, 'I'll see you later.'

'OK, Joey,' she said. 'Thanks.'

As Joey left I picked up a menu and handed it to her.

'Let's order, maybe get some wine,' I said, 'and then you can tell me what this is all about.'

'All right,' she said, 'but I'll be paying the check, since Joey tricked you into coming.'

'I'll pay the check, Abby,' I said. 'I consider that Joey did me a big favor by arranging for me to have dinner with you, instead of him.'

'I can see I'm going to have to watch myself with you, Eddie,' she said. 'You seem to know all the right things to say.'

THREE

I had veal, Abby had chicken.

Once we had dinner in front of us, with a glass of red wine each, I asked Abby to tell me what the problem was.

'I'm being . . . harassed.'

'By who?'

'I don't know,' she said.

'What form is this harassment taking?' I was already thinking that maybe she'd get more help from my private eye buddy, Danny Bardini.

'Phone calls, mail—'

'What did you get in the mail?'

She fidgeted in her chair.

'Years ago, when I was first starting out, I had some . . . pictures taken,' she said, nervously.

'OK, let me stop you,' I said, wanting to ease her discomfort. 'I don't need to know what kind of pictures, and I don't need to see 'em.'

She breathed a sigh of relief and said, 'You're making this a lot easier.'

'That was my intention.'

'Thank you.' She paused for a piece of chicken and I watched with pleasure as she chewed. I don't usually enjoy watching people eat – it's pretty ugly most of the time, people shoveling food into this big hole in their face – but hey, this was Abby Dalton.

'Somebody – probably from my past – sent me a copy of the photo . . . photos. They then called and just sort of . . . gloated.'

'No blackmail?'

'No,' she said, then after a pause, 'not yet, anyway.'

'But you are expecting a demand.'

'Well . . . you tell me. Why else would somebody do this?'

'I don't know,' I said. 'Just to scare you, maybe? I mean, if these photos got out they'd be . . . what? Embarrassing?'

'At the very least.'

'Why would someone do this now?' I asked. 'Because you're a celebrity, and you're on TV?'

'I was on *Hennessy* for three years before doing Joey's show,' she said. 'Why wouldn't they have done it then?'

'Could someone have found these photos, say, accidentally?'

'I suppose . . .'

'Who were they taken by?'

'A professional photographer.'

'And what does he have to say?'

'I don't know,' she said. 'I . . . I haven't spoken with him.'

We paused for a couple of bites each. It was a shame we weren't paying attention to the food. It was very good.

'Joey told me you helped Sammy a couple of years ago when he had a similar problem.'

I didn't know how similar Sammy's situation was, and I couldn't really comment on it, but it did involve – in part – some photos of his wife, May Britt.

'I know you can't talk about that,' she said, 'but I was hoping you would be able to help me, too.'

'Why would you ask me for help and not somebody in Los Angeles?'

'Oh,' she said, 'I didn't tell you. I was born here in Las Vegas, Eddie. The photos were taken here. I think that's really why Joey thought of you.'

Well, that made sense.

After dinner we had dessert – cheesecake for me, a cannoli for her – and discussed the situation further.

'So the photographer was also from here?'

'Yes, he had a studio here. Eddie, I haven't checked, or tried to get in touch with him. I can't – I don't want to—'

'Well,' I said, 'if he's still alive, and workin', I can find him.'

'Then you'll help me?'

'Of course I'll help you, Abby,' I said. 'I mean, I'll do what I can, but you know I'm a pit boss, not a detective.'

She laughed, her eyes lighting up, and said, 'Joey says you're a hell of a detective.'

'Well, I have a friend who is a real detective, and I'll get him to help, too.'

'Wow,' she said. 'I feel a lot better. Lighter.' She looked down at her dessert. 'I think I'll enjoy this.'

'You should,' I said. 'It's very good. You're staying at the Sands?'

'I am, for now,' she said.

'So how did you get started?'

'I was a teen model,' she said. 'Did magazines and album covers until I started working for Roger Corman.'

'You know,' I said, '*Stakeout on Dope Street* and *The Saga of the Viking Women and Their Voyage to the Waters of the Great Sea Serpent* flies in the face of your wholesome image.'

'Oh my God,' she said, putting her hand to her mouth, 'you saw those?'

'I watch TV late at night, sometimes.'

'You know, I hate being called wholesome,' she said, wiping cream from the corner of her mouth with her forefinger. She didn't look very wholesome at that moment. 'And you know what I hate even more than that?'

'What?'

She leaned forward and said, 'I hate being called toothsome.'

'Come on,' I said, 'they usually put the word "beauty" after that.'

'"Toothsome beauty?"' she said. 'That sounds like a left-handed compliment.'

'It's no left-handed compliment to say that you're beautiful.'

'Thank you, sir,' she said, 'but you didn't think so the first time we met, in the Polo Lounge. If I remember correctly, you were with Ava Gardner.'

'I was . . . helpin' her with a situation.'

'Ah,' she said, 'another damsel in distress. You're actually Sir Eddie G., gallant knight.'

'I like to do my part to keep beautiful women happy.'

'Well,' she said, sitting back, 'you've made me a happy girl. A wonderful meal, and you've agreed to help me. I feel much better than I have in weeks.'

'This has been going on for weeks?'

'Eddie,' she said, 'this has been going on for months.'

FOUR

I made notes, specifically concerning the photographer's name and address, and then some dates Abby gave me. After that I paid the bill and we walked out to my car. I opened the passenger-side door for her, watched as she got in with a flash of nylon-covered legs, then got behind the wheel and headed for the Sands.

'How well do you know Joey?' she asked.

'I meet a lot of the celebrities who come to the Sands,' I said. 'Mostly I know them to say hello to, but Joey and I got along from the beginning. Then, a few years ago, he introduced me to Frank and Dean and the others. We became friends.'

'Sounds to me like more than friends, from what Joey says.'

'Really?'

'Yeah,' she said, 'he likes you a lot, says you're a good friend and the guy to see in Vegas.'

'Well, I do what I can to help.'

'When I told him my problem,' she said, 'he told me not to worry, that you could fix it.'

I looked at her for a moment, then back to the road. She was staring straight ahead, and it wasn't easy to pull my gaze away from her lovely profile.

'Abby, I'm going to do my best to help you,' I said, 'but there are no guarantees.'

'I know that, Eddie.'

'You might want to go to the police.'

'No!' I could feel her looking at me. 'No police. I'll . . . I'll just wait and see what you can do.'

'All right,' I said.

'Please, Eddie.' She put her hand on my arm. 'Don't go to the police.'

'Hey,' I said, 'I have no love for the cops, believe me. Besides, that would never be my place. If the police are going to be brought in, it'll be by you. OK?'

'OK.' She dropped her hand. We pretty much rode the rest of the way in silence.

I escorted her into the lobby and watched as she walked to the elevators. Once she got on and the doors closed I went to an elevator myself.

It was well after hours; the Sands' office staff had gone home. The offices were locked, so when I got off on that floor I had my pick of any desk in the reception area. I commandeered one and took out my notebook.

The photographer who shot the photos of Abby was Barney Irwin. Twelve years ago he had an office on South Decatur, near Flamingo Road. I grabbed a nearby phone book. He was still there. Irwin Studios, the 3000 block of South Decatur. It was too late to call, too late to visit. I could drive by in the morning, but I had a shift starting very soon, so I had to trade in my detective hat and put on my pit boss hat.

The Sands casino floor was jumping at midnight, even though Tony Bennett was doing a midnight show in the Copa Room. When the show was over, the floor became even livelier.

The blackjack tables were teeming with regulars, tourists and celebrities. I saw Vic Damone, Jack Jones, Red Skelton, who were all playing other casinos, but gambling at the Sands.

And then I saw him, tall as a telephone pole, and wide as a freeway, coming my way.

'What the hell—' I said.

'Hey, Mr G.,' Jerry Epstein said.

He mauled my hand with his huge paw but gave it back to me not much the worse for wear. The last time I had seen my Brooklyn buddy Jerry was the year before, when we helped Bing Crosby out of a jam that involved horse racing. I didn't usually see Jerry unless there was trouble – and it was usually me in the hot water. I wondered if the tables had turned?

'What are you doin' here?' I asked.

'I'm here with my cousin.'

'Your cousin?'

'Well,' he said, 'my cousin's kid, so I guess that makes him my second cousin. He just turned twenty-one and I told him when he did I'd take him to Vegas. So here we are!'

'Where is he?'

'Playin' craps,' Jerry said. 'He learned all he could about it, developed a system, and now he says he's gonna put it to – what was it? – oh yeah, practical use.'

'Great,' I said. 'Vegas loves system players.'

'I thought maybe you could get away for a drink.'

'Sure thing.' I looked around, waved over a guy named Darrel to stand in for me. 'I'll be in the lounge if something comes up.'

'No problem, boss.'

We got a table in the lounge and ordered two beers. A few losers were sitting at the bar, drowning their sorrows, and a few winners were buying drinks at another table.

'Where are you staying?' I asked.

'Here,' Jerry said. 'Billy and me are sharin' a room.'

'Why didn't you call me?' I asked. 'I would have got you a suite.'

'I ain't lookin for a handout, Mr G.,' Jerry said. 'I told the kid I'd take him to Vegas for his twenty-first birthday. I'm footin' the bill – my present.'

I had to admire him for that. He knew he could get freebies from me whenever he wanted – and he had never asked.

'What're you doin', these days?' he asked me.

'Well,' I said, 'I was minding my own business, until today . . .' I told him about Joey and Abby Dalton, and the photographer.

'I seen her on *Hennessy*,' he said. 'She's some dish.'

'Yeah, she is.'

'You gettin' some of that, Mr G.?'

'No, Jerry, I'm not,' I said. 'I'm just trying to help the lady out.'

'How you gonna do that, exactly?'

'Well, first I'm going to go and see the photographer,' I said. 'He still has a studio in town.'

'That so? When you goin'?'

'Tomorrow morning.'

'You want some company?'

'What about your cousin?'

'I'll leave him at the craps table,' he said. 'Come on, Mr G. You know you'll get into trouble without me.'

I didn't think that was true, but on the other hand he was already in town, and he had offered. So where was the harm in letting him ride shotgun?

'OK, you're on.'

'First you gotta buy me some pancakes in the mornin',' Jerry said.

'I knew this was gonna cost me,' I said.

'Not so much,' he promised. 'Just a coupla stacks.'

FIVE

We touched base some more, finished our beers, and then I had to get back to work.

'I gotta check on the kid anyway, see how much dough he's got left.'

He bought the drinks and then we walked back to the casino floor together.

'Have you seen Mr S., Dino or any of the other guys lately?' he asked.

'Just Joey,' I said. 'Dino was here last month, but nobody since. Frank Jr.'s coming to Tahoe next month to play Harrahs. Frank will probably come in for a few nights.'

We split up at my pit and he asked me what time I was working till.

'Four a.m.'

'Goin' home after that?'

'I'll spend the night here, so I can meet you down here early. Like nine?'

'Good,' he said. 'I'll be hungry by then. You mind if I bring the kid?'

'No, I'd like to meet him,' I said. 'I've always wondered if your size runs in the family.'

'Guess you'll find out tomorrow,' Jerry said. ''Night, Mr G.'

'Good-night, Jerry.'

I spent the night in a room I had used before, when staying over was necessary. In the morning I changed into the clean jeans and T-shirt I kept in my locker. When I got downstairs for breakfast Jerry and his cousin were already there, drinking coffee.

'You're impatient,' I said.

'I'm hungry,' Jerry said. 'Mr G., this is my cousin, Billy.'

Billy was a big boy for twenty-one – not as big as Jerry, but that would probably come with time and age.

'Billy, this is Eddie Gianelli. I told you about him.'

'Yeah, you did,' Billy said. He looked at me with sullen eyes from beneath a shock of wild black hair. 'Hey.'

'Hello,' I said, sitting down. That was the signal for the waitress to come over, a pretty girl I recognized.

'Hello, Ivy.'

'Hey Eddie,' she said, 'they told me they were waiting for you.'

'We're ready,' I said. 'Jerry?'

He ordered a double stack of pancakes, a side of bacon, and more coffee. Billy ordered the same, but he wanted eggs sunny side up, as well. I ordered ham and eggs, toast and coffee.

'Home fries?' she asked.

'Of course,' I said.

'Me, too,' Billy chimed in.

She looked at Jerry.

'Sure, why not?'

'Comin' up,' Ivy said, and hurried away. We all watched.

'Jerry says you have a craps system,' I said to Billy. 'How'd you do last night?'

'I lost,' Billy said, 'but that's part of the system.'

'Losing ain't part of no system I'd trust,' Jerry said.

'It is this one.'

He went on to bend our ear about this system until Ivy came and covered the table with food. Every so often I'd catch Jerry's eyes and he'd give them a roll.

'I wish you luck,' I said to Billy after he'd finished his tutorial. 'We love system players.'

'That's what all the casinos say,' Billy replied. 'That's because you don't think a system can beat you, but this one can.'

'Like I said, good luck.'

He ate like a vacuum cleaner, finishing faster even than Jerry. They both ate two bites to my one.

'I gotta go,' Billy said, when he was done. He jumped up, almost upsetting the table.

'Hey!' Jerry yelled.

'Sorry,' Billy said. 'I gotta get to the tables.'

'Remember what I said,' Jerry told him. 'Don't leave this casino.'

'I won't.' He started away, then stopped short and looked at me. 'Thanks for the breakfast, Mr G.'

'You're welcome,' I said, but he was gone.

Jerry snagged a piece of bacon Billy had left on his plate, then ate the last of his pancakes.

I set the last of my eggs on a piece of toast, added the last of the ham, and shoveled it into my mouth. I still had some potatoes left, and Jerry watched while I ate them with my last slice of toast.

'You ready to go?' he asked.

'Almost,' I said. 'Let me finish my coffee.'

'How do you wanna play this?' he asked. 'Good cop, bad cop? Want me to rough him up?'

'No cops, no roughing up,' I said. 'I just want to talk to 'im.'

'You think he'll remember Miss Dalton?'

'Why not?' I asked. 'How many of the people he's taken pictures of over the years do you think went on to become television stars? And why wouldn't he remember a babe as beautiful as her?'

'I dunno,' Jerry said. 'Maybe he took pictures of lots of pretty girls. Maybe he's a pervert. I hate freaks like that!'

'Well,' I said, 'I'll talk to him first, and if he turns out to be a pervert, then you can rough him up.'

'Good.'

I settled the bill and tipped Ivy generously.

'Thanks, Eddie.'

As we walked out Jerry asked, 'She's pretty. You gettin' some of that, Mr G.?'

'Don't be so interested in my love life, Jerry,' I said.

SIX

Jerry drove my Caddy. I'd never seen his big hands be as gentle with anything else as he was with the steering wheel of my car.

We parked down the street from the studio and walked to it. It had a glass front, with a single glass door. In the windows were dozens of photos, presumably taken by Barney Irwin. And smack in the middle was a framed photo of a young Abby Dalton.

'I guess that answers the question of whether or not he'll remember her,' I said, pointing.

Jerry leaned in to look closer at the photo that almost looked like it belonged in a yearbook. Her hair piled up on her head, her long neck leading down to bare shoulders.

'I think she looks better now,' Jerry said, straightening up.

'I agree.'

We went to the door of Irwin Studios and pushed it open.

The inside had a musty smell, and a thin layer of dust on everything. Apparently, Irwin Studios didn't do much business anymore. Come to think of it, all the photos in the window had an aged look to them.

'What a dump,' Jerry said.

I looked around. It hadn't always been a dump. I could see the rug had cost a pretty penny in its day. Also the wall paneling. There were different size and style picture frames on shelves, but some of them were tarnished.

There was a curtained doorway leading to either a back room or a hallway. The curtain was faded, red and threadbare.

'Is there a bell for us to ring?' Jerry asked.

'I don't see one, but why don't we just take a peek behind curtain number three and see what we find?'

Jerry looked around and said, 'There's only one curtain.'

'Jerry—'

'I'm kiddin' ya, Mr G.,' he said. 'You of all people know I ain't that dumb.'

'Yeah, I do know that. Come on.'

We went to the curtain and I pushed it aside to see a hallway.

I led the way, with Jerry's bulk crowding behind me. About halfway back we began to hear a voice.

'That's it sweetie, that's it,' a man said. 'Now stick it out. Yeah! That's it. Work it! Work it for daddy!' At the end of the hall we could see flashes of light coming from another doorway.

We got to the end of the hall, found another threadbare curtain, this one blue. I parted it just enough to look inside. We saw a thickset bald man with a camera, clicking off shots of a naked girl on a small stage. After each shot a spent flash bulb would pop from the camera and hit the floor, and he'd load a new one. She was busty and blonde, showgirl material, and at the moment she was working it for daddy, pushing out her chubby boobs and butt. I always wondered how women could do that without breaking their backs.

'How do they do that—' Jerry started to whisper.

'I know!'

'Whataya wanna do?'

'Follow my lead.'

'OK.'

I pushed the curtain aside and walked through. Jerry was so close behind me that he clipped my heels.

'Sorry,' he whispered.

'Oh!' the girl said when she saw us, but did nothing to try to cover up. Instead, she seemed to appreciate the audience, and Jerry appreciated the show.

'Nice tits,' he said.

'Thank you.'

The photographer turned around. He was in his sixties, with a gleaming bald head. His once powerful physique had gone to seed, but still had powerful shoulders, while his belly hung over his belt. He was wearing a yellow polo shirt, powder blue trousers, with a white belt and shoes.

'Who are you?' he demanded.

'My name's Eddie Gianelli,' I said. 'I'm from the Sands.'

'Oh,' the girl said, again. 'Is this the guy you told me about, Barney?' she asked, in a baby doll voice.

'Huh?' Barney Irwin said. 'Oh, no, baby, he ain't the guy.'

He must have already promised her she'd meet a guy who would give her a job. Sorry, I thought, not me.

'Whataya want?' he asked me, but he was looking past me, at Jerry.

'We need to talk.'

'About what?'

'Abby Dalton.'

'Abby . . .' He turned to the girl. 'Get dressed, baby.'

'Are we done, Barney?'

'Yeah, baby, we're done.'

'When will I get to meet—'

'Get dressed!' he snapped. 'I'll talk to you later.'

'OK, Barney.'

She stepped down from the stage and trotted off toward another door, and through. We all watched her jiggle until she was gone, then looked back at each other.

'You remember Abby Dalton, don't you, Mr Irwin?' I asked.

'She was Marlene Wasden when I knew her,' Irwin said. 'A pretty little thing. You can see her picture in my window.'

'But she's a TV star now,' I said. 'Famous.'

'So she is.' He walked to a table and set his camera down on it. 'What's that got to do with me?' He started walking around the room, stooping to pick up the spent bulbs.

'What was that girl's name?' I asked.

He straightened and looked at me. 'Who? Jenny?' He jerked his thumb in the direction of the door the girl had gone through.

'You ever take pictures of other girls like the ones you were takin' of Jenny?' I asked.

'Sure,' Barney said. 'I got connections. I can get them jobs at the casinos.'

'As what? Cigarette girls?'

'Show girls,' he said. 'That's why they come to me. That's why they pose.' He dropped all the bulbs into a trash can.

'And what about Abby? Or Marlene? Did she pose for pictures like those?'

'Like those?' Barney asked. 'No, she was classy, even as a teenager.'

'So that means no naked pictures of her?'

Irwin turned to look at me.

'Why are you interested?' he asked. 'Why should I talk to you about that?'

'I'm just askin' questions, Barney.'

'Yeah, but why?' Irwin asked. 'Say, who sent you here? Who gave you my name?'

'Ask anybody in Vegas who takes the best cheesecake pictures,' I said. 'Don't they say Barney Irwin?'

Irwin frowned. 'You tryin' to do a stroke job on me?'

'Me?' I said. 'Stroke the great Barney Irwin?'

'Aw, whataya want here?' Irwin said, growing annoyed. 'I got work to do.'

'Got another girl comin' in?' I asked. 'Another young girl to make get naked in front of you?'

'Hey, I'm an artist,' Irwin said. 'All artists use girls as models.'

'Yeah,' Jerry said, 'but most artists got talent.'

'Hey, I got talent,' Irwin said. 'I been in this business a long time.'

'Yeah,' Jerry said, 'we can tell that from all the dust on everything in here.'

'Oh, that?' Irwin said. 'Yeah, I got a woman who comes in – only she's been sick.'

'You got any copies of the photos you took of Abby Dalton, Barney?'

Irwin hesitated, then said, 'That was a long time ago.'

'Does that mean no?'

'I'd have to look.'

'I tell you what,' I said. 'If you find any, I'll buy them from you. Top dollar.'

Irwin got a greedy look in his eyes.

'Top dollar?'

'For every photo. And the negative.'

'I'll have to look,' he said, again.

I took out a business card and placed it on a table.

'Give me a call at the Sands when you find them.'

'And what about my girls? Like Jenny? What about her? Can you get her a job in your show?'

'It's not my show,' I said, 'but I'll see what I can do.'

'I got lots of girls like her.'

'I'll bet you do.'

'I got plenty of pictures of them.'

'Just the pictures of Abby Dalton for now, Barney,' I said. 'Let's start there.'

SEVEN

We left the studio and walked to the car. Along the way we passed a buxom redhead walking quickly toward the place.

'Next,' Jerry said.

'Probably.'

'I coulda squeezed him, ya know,' Jerry said.

'I know it, Jerry. Let's see what my offer gets us first.' I had the uncomfortable feeling I had played it wrong.

'You really think he'll sell you nudie pictures of Miss Dalton?'

'I don't know,' I said. 'It depends on how greedy he is. If he's the one harassing it's more likely he'll come up with a bunch of cheesecake photos, just for the money, but no nudes.'

'But you said nobody asked Miss Dalton for any money, yet.'

'That's right.'

'So maybe it ain't him.'

'Even if he's not the one contacting her,' I said, 'he's still the one who took the photos. She didn't say anything about posing for anyone else.'

'What about pictures from movies?' Jerry asked.

'She hasn't been naked in any movies.'

'Yeah, but maybe on the set, or in her dressing room? Maybe somebody caught her when she wasn't looking?'

'Maybe.'

We got to the Caddy and got in, Jerry behind the wheel. He started the car and pulled away from the curb.

'Where to?' he asked.

'Back to the Sands.'

'What about somethin' to eat?'

'It's not lunch time,' I said.

'I was thinkin' about a snack.'

'We just had breakfast.'

'That was a couple of hours ago,' he said.

I gave in and directed Jerry to a diner. I had coffee while he polished off a burger, fries and a large Coke.

'I got an idea,' he said.

'What?'

'Why don't we take a look in Irwin's studio before he has a chance to get rid of anything.'

'You mean break in?'

He nodded. 'Tonight.'

'He might have gotten rid of everything by then.'

'Well then, right after he closes up,' Jerry said.

'He might still take the photos home, or destroy them. I think I might've played this wrong, Jerry.'

'All we need to do is have somebody watch him,' Jerry said, 'then follow him. See what he leaves with. Once we get inside we should be able to tell if he burned anything.'

'I don't know,' I said. 'Breaking and entering . . .'

'We done worse before.'

'I know it.'

'What about the private eye?' he asked. 'Can he watch him?'

He meant Danny Bardini, my buddy the private eye.

'I'll give him a call, see if he's around and available.'

'Then we'll do it?'

'Yeah, sure,' I said. 'Why not? Let's take a look and see what ol' Barney's got.'

'When Danny finds out where he lives, we can check that out, too.'

'Jerry,' I said, 'why don't we handle one break-in at a time.'

EIGHT

When we got back to the Sands, Jerry went looking for his cousin, and I got to a phone and called Danny's office.

'Hey, big boy,' Penny said. 'You haven't been around in a while.'

'Well,' I said, 'that either means I've been busy, or I've been staying out of trouble. Is he around?'

'He is,' she said. 'I'll put you through.'

Penny was Danny's secretary, but she wanted to be more – both professionally, and personally. Danny trusted very few people. I was one, Penny was fighting to become another.

'Hey, pit boss,' he said. 'What's up?'

'Danny, I need your talent.'

'As what?'

'As a PI, doofus,' I said. 'What else?'

'I thought maybe you needed help with your love life.'

'My love life is fine,' I said, although I almost said, 'What love life?'

'Whataya need?'

'You know who Abby Dalton is?'

'Do I?' he said. 'She's that dish who plays Joey Bishop's wife. And she used to be on *Hennessy*.'

'You've been watching a lot of TV lately.'

'Yeah, well . . . never mind that,' he said, because following that up might lead to questions about *his* love life. 'You tellin' me I'm gonna meet Abby Dalton?'

'Maybe,' I said. 'Here's the deal.'

I gave it to him step by step, and he listened quietly, didn't speak until I was finished.

'You let the big guy talk you into breakin' into the studio?'

'Yep, that's what happened.'

'Jesus . . . whataya need me for. A lookout?'

'I need you to get over there and watch him,' I said. 'I want to know if he leaves with anything. And I want to know where he goes. And where he lives.'

'Is that all of it?'

'For now.'

'You don't want my help with the break in?'

'No, I think Jerry and I can handle that part.'

'What about where he lives? You gonna break in there, too?'

'Well . . . if we don't find what we're looking for at the studio.'

'OK,' Danny said, 'so when I follow him home I'll scope it out, look for the best ways in.'

'That'd be great.'

'And when do I meet the luscious Miss Dalton?'

'Somewhere along the way,' I said, 'I'm sure that'll happen.'

'No, no, no,' he said, 'we gotta agree that it *will* happen.'

'OK,' I said, 'somewhere along the way it *will* happen.'

'You know,' he said, 'sometimes bein' friends with you has perks . . .'

Yeah, I thought, like meeting Marilyn Monroe, Ava Gardner, and now Abby.

'. . . but sometimes it don't.'

Oh yeah, like being kidnapped and tied up in a basement for days, and almost getting killed.

'So I guess you'll have to weigh up the pros and cons,' I said.

'Oh, I did that a long time ago, buddy,' he said, 'and you came out on top. Give me the address of the studio.'

Irwin Studios had its hours on the door, printed on a faded card. The day being a Wednesday he closed at five p.m. We arrived at five fifteen and parked, around the corner this time.

'We can't go in the front,' Jerry said. 'Even an amateur like you knows that.'

'I'm an amateur?' I asked. 'When did you become a professional burglar?'

'I'm in what you call a related profession, Mr G.'

'I see.'

'We gotta go around the back.'

We found an alley that led behind the strip of buildings that included the studio. There were dumpsters back there, and a few of the buildings had docks for deliveries. Lucky for us, the address numbers were on the walls.

'This is it,' Jerry said. It was a green metal door, which meant that breaking it down was out of the question, even for Jerry.

'Now what?' I asked. 'A window?'

'No, I'm gonna try somethin',' Jerry said. He took out what looked like a case for eyeglasses. 'Lock picks,' he said. 'I got 'em a few weeks ago, and I been practicin'.'

He got down on one knee and inserted the tools into the lock. It takes precision to pick a lock, and I was surprised he could even attempt it with fingers the size of his.

After fifteen minutes I asked, 'How much longer is this gonna take?'

'I almost got it.'

'Well, come on,' I urged him. 'It's starting to get dark.'

'Don't worry,' He said, without looking at me. 'I brought a flashlight.'

I looked at him. He was wearing jeans and a windbreaker.

'Where the hell are you carrying a flashlight?' I asked.

He paused long enough to go into his pocket and show it to me.

It looked like a pen in his big hand. He put it back and returned his attention to the lock.

After twenty minutes he said, 'Got it.'

'Good.'

He reached for the door and I put my hand out to stop him.

'What's wrong?'

'I don't want to find any bodies inside.'

'Why would we find a body?'

'I'm just putting it out there,' I said. 'I mean, we have a history.'

'No bodies, Mr G.,' he assured me.

'OK.'

He opened the door and we went inside.

NINE

It was dusk but dark inside. In another half hour it would be genuine night.

We were in a hallway, but not the same one as last time. Jerry took out his pen light and turned it on. The beacon was remarkably bright for its size.

'We gotta find an office,' Jerry said. 'That's where he'll keep his files.'

We moved down the hall, with me following closely behind. I was careful not to step on his heels.

Jerry used his light to find the office, off the hallway we were in.

'We're in luck,' he said.

'Why?'

'No windows,' he said. 'We can turn on a light.'

He found a desk lamp, switched it on, then flicked off his flashlight and put it back in his pocket. The lamp was one of those with a green glass shade, most of the light being directed to the desk top. But we were still able to see the rest of the room pretty well. The desk itself was cheap metal, with many dents and one leg shorter than the other three. The top was a mess of papers and photos. Along one wall was a mismatched collection of metal file cabinets which, I assumed, contained files collected over many years.

A layer of dust covered everything, but it enabled us to see which parts of the room Irwin used the most.

'Look here,' Jerry said. 'These two cabinets have got his hand prints all over 'em.'

'And the desk,' I said. 'Let's get started.'

I took the desk, and Jerry started on the cabinets. I sat in Irwin's rickety chair and started rifling the drawers. There were two on the left, two on the right, and a smaller, center one. I started on the left, found one drawer full of papers. I leafed through them, but didn't find anything interesting. The top left drawer had something, though – a .38 revolver. I didn't touch it, closed the drawer and started on the right. More papers, some cheesecake photos of what looked like half a dozen pretty young girls. They were all smiling vacantly into the camera while showing lots of leg or cleavage. The top drawer yielded a half-eaten sandwich – tuna, from the smell – and some rotten fruit that had been in there for a while.

I only had the center drawer left.

'I got lots of pictures,' Jerry said, 'but none of Miss Dalton.'

'Any nudes at all?'

'No,' he said, 'just cheesecake.'

'Yeah, me, too.'

More papers, some note paper that he'd scribbled on. I was about to close the drawer when a name jumped out at me.

Sinatra.

I took the note paper out and looked at it. This was written on it:

Nov. 22.
Sinatra.
Keenan & Amsler.
Barry.
Johnny.
Canoga Park.

'Anything?' Jerry asked.

'Not about Abby,' I said.

'Then what?'

'I don't know,' I said. I folded the sheet and put it in my pocket. 'Maybe we can figure it out later. Let's keep looking.'

I went through the rest of the drawer, but found nothing.

'Still got another cabinet over there,' Jerry said, pointing.

'I'm on it.'

I got up and moved to the cabinet. There were half a dozen more, but the dust revealed they hadn't been touched in a while.

I started at the bottom, closing each drawer after I finished. We didn't want to leave any indication that we'd been there.

I found much of what Jerry was finding, and what I had found in the desk, files with girls' names, cheesecake photos.

'Mr G., he must be keepin' the nudies someplace else,' Jerry said. 'Like at home.'

'You're probably right,' I said, closing the top drawer. 'We better get out of here. I'll call Danny and see what he's got for us.'

Jerry went to the desk and pulled the chain on the lamp, plunging the room into darkness. Seconds later his pen light went on and pointed the way to the door.

TEN

Outside, with the door locked behind us, we got into the Caddy. Jerry asked if he should drive back to the Sands.

'No,' I said, 'my place. You can spend the night. In the morning I'll pack a bag and we'll head over to the Sands. I need to put some fresh clothes in my locker.'

'What about your pit?'

'I'm not scheduled to work tonight.'

We pulled into the driveway of my little house. I opened the front door, and Jerry went directly to the kitchen, got two cans of Piels from the frig. He opened them both with an opener and then handed me one.

'I want to show you something,' I said. I took the piece of paper from my jacket pocket and showed it to him.

'What does it mean?' he asked.

'I don't know,' I said. 'It was in his center drawer. Do you know any of the names, other than Frank's?'

'Well, Irwin, that's the photographer's name.'

'Why would he write his own name like that?' I asked. 'I'd say it was a brother, or cousin.'

'And these other names? Keenan and Amsler? I never heard of 'em.'

'Neither have I.' I took the paper back from him. 'Could be nothing, I guess.'

Jerry finished his beer and said, 'We gotta get somethin' to eat.'

'How about a pizza?'

The big guy made a face. 'In Vegas?'

'You're right.' Pizza in Vegas was terrible, especially when you grew up in Brooklyn.

'How about Chinks?' he suggested.

'Sounds good. There's a take-out place near here. Their menu is in that drawer by the sink. I'm gonna call Danny.'

I went into the living room and dialed Danny's home number. It was too late to try his office. He didn't answer. I went back to the kitchen.

'No answer,' I said. 'He must still be watching Irwin.'

'Why? You only wanted to know where he lived? Why's he still watchin'?'

'I guess we'll find out when he calls us. You pick what you want from that?' I pointed to the menu he was holding.

'Yeah,' Jerry said. 'Here.'

'Why don't you call it in? I'll eat whatever you order.'

He looked crestfallen.

'My food?'

'Sorry,' I said. 'What was I thinking?' I forgot that Jerry didn't like to share his food. 'Order me some spare ribs, and the pepper steak.'

'Fried rice?'

'Of course.'

'Gotcha.'

This time he went into the living room to use the phone. I put some water in a kettle and set it on the stove for tea then sat at the kitchen table to finish my beer and give our evening's activities some thought.

The table was covered with Chinese food cartons. Both Jerry and I were inept with chopsticks, so we each used a fork.

'How can you manipulate lock picks, but not chopsticks?' I asked.

'Nothin' beats lock picks for a lock,' Jerry said. 'I mean, when ya don't have a key. And nothin' beats a fork for eatin'.' He paused a moment, then added, 'Besides, chopsticks are stupid.'

As I picked up my last egg roll, I couldn't disagree with him.

ELEVEN

Jerry slept on the sofa. It was a large one and almost accommodated him. But he'd slept there before and knew how to maneuver it. Besides, he could sleep on a picket fence.

I lay awake for a while, wondering if the words on the list had anything to do with Abby Dalton, then decided they didn't. It had to be something totally unconnected. I was just making things more complicated. We simply had to find those photos and negatives, and reveal Irwin to be the culprit.

I finally fell asleep, wondering why Barney hadn't asked for any money. Or should that be . . . yet?

Food was never as big a part of my life as it was when Jerry was around. The next morning I packed a small bag and we went to a diner near my house, where we had eaten breakfast a few times before. He ordered pancakes. I ordered a Spanish omelet.

'What about French toast?' I asked.

'A poor substitute for pancakes.'

'Waffles?'

He shrugged. 'Same thing.'

I left him alone after that and let him eat his pancakes.

I had called Danny's home number before we left my house and gotten no answer. Then I called his office, but it was too early. I was starting to worry about him, and having flashbacks to when I had asked him to go to LA with me, and he'd disappeared. We were lucky to get him back that time.

Jerry drove us down the strip, past the marquees that announced Alan King was at the Riviera, Louie Prima was playing the Desert Inn. As we made the turn into the Sands I saw that Nat King Cole was at the Flamingo. The Sands' marquee said 'A Place in the Sun' and announced Tony Bennett.

When we got out of the car Jerry said, 'I'm gonna find Billy, and also go to my room for a shower. Let me know when you hear from the PI guy.'

'I will.'

I went to my locker first and put the fresh clothes away. When I came back up I was walking through the lobby of the hotel when one of the girls behind the desk waved at me.

'I've got some messages for you, Eddie,' she said.

I didn't remember her name, so I said, 'Thanks, sweetie.'

She handed me the slips. She was new, a pretty brunette. I'd have to ask somebody her name, and then make a point of remembering it.

One slip was from Danny. It said he'd meet me in the Garden Room at noon. I checked my watch. It was just after ten.

The second message was from Barney Irwin, and only had a call back number on it. I could have gone to the desk to use the phone, but I decided to use a pay phone, instead. More privacy. I got into a booth, deposited a dime and dialed the number.

'Irwin Studios.'

'Barney? This is Eddie Gianelli.'

'I got what you want, Gianelli,' Irwin said, 'but it's gonna cost you.'

This was more like it.

'I told you I'd pay,' I said. 'I'll come and pick the photos up.'

'Not here,' Irwin said. 'There's a bar on Decatur called Clipper's. Meet me there at six tonight.'

'I'll be there.'

'Leave your big dog home,' Irwin said, and hung up before I could respond.

I came out of the phone booth and walked smack dab into my boss, Jack Entratter.

'There you are!' he said. 'I've been lookin' for you.'

'I'm early, Jack,' I said. 'My shift's not till later.'

'I mean I been lookin' for you for days, Eddie,' he said.

'Yesterday was my day off.'

'Always an excuse,' he said. 'Come up to my office with me.'

'What's it about?'

'Let's wait until we get upstairs.'

Obediently, I followed Entratter to the elevators, then to his office. When we walked in his girl was at her desk and gave me one of her looks of disdain. I had never gotten into it with her about why she disliked me. I guess it just wasn't that important to me.

'Close the door, Eddie.'

I closed it. Jack was behind his desk, so I went and sat across from him.

'What's up, Jack?'

'I like to know what's goin' on in my place, Eddie.'

'I know that.'

'Your buddy Jerry Epstein is in town. In fact, he's in this hotel.'

'I know that, too.'

'What's he doin' here?'

'He brought his nephew to Vegas for his twenty-first birthday.'

'What?'

I shrugged. 'That's it. It's a family thing.'

'What's his nephew doin'?'

'Playin' craps,' I said. 'He's got a system.'

Jack settled back in his chair. 'God bless system players.'

'I know, that's what I told them. But he insists it's gonna work.'

'OK, so what's Jerry gonna do while his nephew is gambling?'

'Cousin,' I corrected. Here was my chance to tell Jack what I was doing for Abby Dalton, except she didn't want it to be generally known. Jack had always told me he wanted the guys to be happy when they were here. That usually meant Frank and Dino, but I extended it to mean Sammy and Joey, too. (Peter Lawford could fend for himself. I never liked Lawford, and now he was on the outs with Frank.)

'I guess he's gonna play the ponies and eat.'

'That's it?'

'No,' I said, 'I'll probably have some meals with him. After all, we're friends.'

'Yeah, well . . . OK.'

'That's it?'

'No,' Entratter said, 'I wanna talk to you about some of the new dealers. You got time?'

'Sure, I got time, Jack,' I said, even though I was chafing at the bit to get out of there and call Abby. 'That's my job.'

'OK, then,' he said. 'You want coffee. I'll have my girl bring it in.'

'Yeah, but don't tell her it's for me,' I said. 'She'll spit in it.'

'She ain't gonna spit in it, Eddie,' he said. 'She knows I gotta drink it, too.'

'Yeah, well . . .'

He buzzed her and said into the intercom, 'Coffee, please, and two cups.'

'Yes, sir.'

'OK, Eddie,' Entratter said, 'let's talk about that kid – what's his name . . .?'

TWELVE

I spent an hour and a half with Entratter, and in that time I saved three jobs, and got two guys fired. Tough luck. As dealers, they sucked.

'OK,' Jack finally said, 'that's it, then.'

'I'll see you later, Jack. I got some things to do before my shift.'

I got up and headed for the door.

'Eddie.'

'Yeah?' I turned at the door.

'Keep an eye on your big buddy, huh? Trouble follows him.'

'I don't think that's fair, Jack,' I said. 'But I'll keep an eye on him.'

'OK, thanks.'

He grabbed some papers from his desk as I went out the door. His girl and I avoided each other's eyes as I walked out into the hall.

I took the elevator down to the lobby, then went over to the house phones.

I called Abby, who was very anxious to hear from me.

'I saw Irwin yesterday, and have an appointment with him tonight to buy some photos.'

'You mean . . . *the* photos?'

'I hope so,' I said. 'He didn't mention specifics yesterday, or this morning when I spoke to him. I guess I'll find out when I get there.'

'I have some cash,' she said. 'I took it out of the bank after we spoke. Do you want to come up and get it?'

I almost said yes, then remembered Danny was waiting for me in the Garden Room.

'Why don't you meet me down here in the Garden Room at noon?' I asked. 'I want you to meet someone who's helping us out.'

'You told someone else?' she asked.

'Only someone I trust completely,' I said. Now it struck me I better not tell her about Jerry. 'Don't worry.'

'All right. I'll meet you there.'

'Good. I'll see you in a little while.'

'Thank you, Eddie.'

'Thank me when we get this whole thing settled.'

'I'm thanking you just for trying to help,' she said.

'You're welcome, Abby. See you soon.'

I hung up, checked my watch. It was eleven forty-five. Just enough time for Abby to get herself together and come down.

I went directly to the Garden Room.

I got there first, grabbed a booth, had coffee waiting on the table by the time Danny got there at five minutes to noon.

'Thanks,' Danny said gratefully, when I filled a mug for him. He sat opposite me, with his back to the door.

'Tried to call you a few times,' I said.

'Been out,' Danny said. 'I followed your man home last night, then had some work to do on another case.' He leaned forward and added, 'A paying case.'

'Hey,' I said, sounding wounded, 'I'm gonna pay.'

'Oh yeah? When?'

Abby walked in at that moment, so I said, 'Right now,' and stood up.

She came alongside the table and I said, 'Abby Dalton, I'd like you to meet Danny Bardini.'

Danny jumped to his feet, almost upsetting the table. He grabbed it to keep it from falling over, then stood up straight and stared.

'I'm glad to meet you Mr Bardini.'

'Um, me, too, Miss Dalton.'

'Have a seat,' I said, and Abby slid in so she could sit next to me. She was wearing a tight sweater, a skirt and high heels. Her hair was piled on top of her head, leaving her long, graceful neck bare.

Danny sat, giving me a hard look for not warning him. He was wearing a rumpled suit that looked as if he'd spent the night in it. I was casual and clean in a T-shirt, jeans and windbreaker.

'Abby, Danny is one of my best friends, and also happens to be a private detective. He's agreed to help us.'

'Oh, that's wonderful,' she said. She gave him a look that would weaken any man's knees. 'I'll pay you, of course.'

'Nonsense,' Danny said. 'I'm happy to help.' Like me, Danny's Brooklyn accent kind of went and hid when he was around beautiful women.

'Coffee?' I asked Abby.

'Yes, please.'

'Something to eat?' I asked, as I poured.

'No, I was up early and had breakfast before I went to the bank. I have some cash here—' She started to go into her purse, but I stopped her.

'We have time for that,' I said. 'Let's hear what Danny has for us, first.'

'Well,' Danny said, 'I picked your man up around two in the afternoon. He was in his studio and didn't leave till five. He had a brown envelope with him, about eight-and-a-half by ten. I followed him home, a dump on Spring Mountain Road between a couple of strip clubs. He went in and didn't come out. I sat on him until eleven, when all the lights went out.'

'What about the next morning?' I asked.

'I thought of that,' Danny said. 'I went back this morning about seven a.m. He left the house at eight. He was carrying a brown envelope.'

'He's supposed to meet me at a bar tonight with the photos,' I said.

'Well,' Danny said, 'maybe that's what he was carrying. Or maybe he'll go back to the house to get them, and he was carrying something entirely different. Somebody's baby pictures.'

'Why would he do that?' I asked. 'The bar's practically around the corner from his place. That doesn't sound right.'

'Then the photos are either in that envelope, in his house, or still at his studio.'

'We searched the whole studio pretty good,' I pointed out.

'Look for false bottoms in drawers, false walls, a safe?' he asked.

'No.'

Danny shrugged. 'Then the stuff could still be there, somewhere.'

'Danny, you said his house has strip clubs around it?' I asked.

'Yup.'

'Not so busy during the day.'

'Nope.'

He knew what I was thinking, but neither of us said it in front of Abby. Jerry and I could break into the house while he was at work, take a look around.

'OK,' I said. 'OK. You want something to eat?' I asked Danny.

'I could use something.'

I looked at Abby.

'I'll just have more coffee,' she said. 'I've got to watch my figure.'

I looked at Danny, hoping he wouldn't say, 'We can do that.' He didn't.

'Yeah, me, too,' I said, and waved the waitress over. Danny ordered lunch. Abby and I drank coffee while he ate.

THIRTEEN

After Danny finished his lunch, Abby asked, 'What about the money?'

'How much do you have with you?' I asked.

'Five thousand,' she said.

'Give it to me.'

She opened her purse, which seemed just large enough to accommodate the white envelope she took out. She handed it to me and I could feel the thickness of the wad of cash inside.

'Will it be enough?' she asked.

'We'll see,' I said. 'If they're not the photos we're looking for, I won't even make the deal.'

'I would like . . . all the photos he has,' she said, haltingly. 'I mean, even just . . . modeling photos.'

'All right,' I said. 'I'll get whatever he brings with him.'

'Thank you. I have to go, now. I'm supposed to meet Joey for some publicity for the show.'

I got up to let her out, and Danny got to his feet, as well.

'We'll talk later, Abby,' I said.

'Thank you, Eddie.' She turned to Danny. 'And thank you for your help, Mr Bardini.'

'I'm happy to be of service, Miss Dalton.'

She smiled at him, and left the coffee shop.

After she left, Danny and I sat back down. I poured more coffee for each of us.

'You'll need back-up for this meet, tonight,' Danny said.

'He's just a middle-aged photographer, Danny,' I said. 'I don't think I'll have any trouble.'

'He might have some friends who aren't so middle-aged.'

'I'll take Jerry.'

'You said he told you not to bring Jerry,' Danny pointed out. 'Besides, he's seen Jerry. He's never seen me. I'll get to the bar early and get myself a ringside seat.'

'All right,' I said. 'Thanks.'

'And keep Jerry away from there.'

'I'll tell him.'

'Make sure he understands,' Danny said. 'You don't need him rushing in and queering the deal.'

'It's a simple swap, Danny.'

'I've seen many simple swaps go wrong, Eddie,' Danny said, dead serious. 'Believe me, you can't be too careful.'

'Yeah, OK,' I said. 'We'll do it your way.'

'For a change, you mean,' he said.

'Yeah,' I agreed, 'for a change.'

Together we walked out to the street. The sun was bright, and the day was busy already, valets running back and forth, parking customers' cars. We watched women exit their automobiles in flashes of nylon and heels, men in suits and fedoras. People dressed to gamble in those days. Many of the women wore their Jackie Kennedy influences: dark glasses, shift dresses, pea coats. At night, when the sun went down, they'd put on white gloves, pearls, designer dresses and gowns from Cassini to Valentino to Givenchy just to attend the shows, and then gamble late into the night.

I didn't usually get to rub shoulders with women like that, not while I was in the pit. When they played blackjack they had their men right next to them, guarding their women like possessions. Even the pros, who were on the arms of the men who had rented them, dressed the part.

Danny and me, we still had Brooklyn inside of us. We were more comfortable in some of the downtown casinos, where the people were more concerned with the actual gambling than with what they wore while they tossed the dice.

'My car's in the back,' Danny said.

'We could have gone out that way.'

'I'll walk around,' he said. 'I wanted to see some of the pretty people.'

'Where will we meet after?'

'Downtown,' he said. 'The Horseshoe. In the coffee shop.'

'OK.'

He put his hand on my arm.

'Don't take this lightly, OK?' he asked. 'If Irwin's a blackmailer, then he's more than just a middle-aged photographer. And if . . . if you're planning on breaking into his house, I don't wanna know about it. Got it?'

I nodded, and watched Danny as he worked his way between the cars, and then rounded the corner. Despite what he said, I couldn't help thinking Barney Irwin was just a wannabe Hugh Hefner, out for a fast buck or an even faster fuck.

I went back inside to find Jerry. I had to tell him I didn't need him that night, and make him believe it.

FOURTEEN

The club on one side of Irwin's house was called The Diamond Club. The other was called Foxy's. The house was a rundown, one-story wood A-frame.

'We better pull around back, Mr G.,' Jerry said.

'Go ahead.'

He whipped the Caddy around to the back and cut the engine. As we got out he looked at the two buildings.

'No doors or windows on this side,' he said. 'Nobody'll see us.'

'You gonna pick the locks again?'

'This cracker box?' Jerry asked. 'I'll just slip the lock.'

He used a piece of celluloid to slip the lock and open the door. Nobody would ever be able to tell.

We were in the kitchen.

'He's got to have an office here,' I said. 'Maybe a darkroom in the basement.'

'I'll take the basement,' Jerry said.

'OK,' I said, 'I'll snoop around up here.'

The living room was cheaply furnished; the linoleum had worn through to show the wood floor beneath it. The furniture was marked with cigarette burns, rings, scratches. I didn't find an office or a desk on the first floor. As I got to the basement steps Jerry called up, 'Hey, Mr G. You better get down here.'

I went down the steps, found Jerry standing among some file cabinets, trays of chemicals, and clotheslines for drying photos. There was a black light in the ceiling.

'This is where he develops his photos,' Jerry said. 'And look here.' He opened the top drawer of a file cabinet, reached inside and came out with a handful of photos. He spread them out on the table. They were all of nude, young girls who looked anywhere from sixteen to nineteen. Some of the pictures themselves were older than others.

'The whole drawer?' I asked.

'Filled to the brim.'

'Any of Abby?'

'Not that I can see.'

'We'll have to go through them all,' I said.

He shrugged and said, 'OK with me.'

We started leafing through photos of skinny girls, full-bodied girls, tall, short, blondes, brunettes, redheads. Hundreds of photos, but none of Abby Dalton.

'He's got 'em,' I said. 'He's got 'em with 'im.'

'So he is gonna sell them to you tonight,' Jerry said.

'Maybe,' I said. 'I'll find out when I see him.'

'I'll come along.'

'He doesn't want you there, Jerry,' I said. 'If he sees you, he might not show up.'

'He won't see me.'

'Look, Jerry,' I said, 'Danny's gonna be inside. Irwin's never seen him.'

'I'll be outside, Mr G.,' he said. 'Irwin won't catch on and neither will the dick. I won't come in unless there's shootin'.'

'You didn't bring a gun with you on this trip, did you?'

'No,' Jerry said, 'but I can get one.'

'Look, Jerry, I'll tell you what I told Danny. This guy's a middle-aged photographer, not a hard guy. There's not gonna be any shooting.'

'And I'll bet I'm tellin' you what the dick told you,' Jerry said. 'You never know what kind of a guy somebody is. Sometimes, you find out too late. So it's better to be ready.'

'He didn't tell me that.'

'Well, he should've.'

'He told me a simple swap is not always a simple swap.'

'He's right about that.'

I looked down at the photos in my hand.

'What do we do now?' Jerry asked.

'I don't think we're gonna find any photos of Abby here,' I said, 'but let's keep looking, just in case.'

'Fine by me.'

We spent a good hour searching the whole house. We found more nudes in a bedroom closet, in a cardboard box, but they were more than nude. They were porn, showing men and women engaged in many different types and positions of sexual activity.

'Man, that's gotta hurt,' Jerry said, of one photo in particular.

'These are not just photos,' I said. 'They look like stills.'

'From blue movies, you mean?'

I nodded.

'But this isn't what we're interested in. Let's put 'em back and go back downstairs.'

On the way down I said, 'I'm thinking we missed something in his studio.'

'Maybe he just kept the pictures of Miss Dalton all someplace else,' Jerry said. 'Maybe he's really gonna give 'em all to you tonight.'

'You believe that?'

'No. Blackmailers are the worst. They're never satisfied.'

'We've got to satisfy this one, Jerry.'

'I'm ready, Mr G.,' Jerry said. 'I love squeezin' blackmailers.'

'Well, let me talk to him tonight, and then we'll see about squeezin' him.'

'With me outside and the dick inside, we gotcha covered.'

'I know,' I said. 'I appreciate it.'

'We gotta clean up here.' We were in the basement again, the nude photos still spread out on a table. 'Or he'll know we was here.'

'No,' I said.

'What?'

'I want to take all these with us.'

'All of 'em?'

'Oh, yeah,' I said. 'If he's plannin' to blackmail anybody else, I want to throw a monkey wrench into the works.'

Jerry went back to the file drawer and looked inside.

'We got negatives here, Mr G.'

'Good,' I said. 'We'll take all the copies, and the negatives.'

'Then he'll really know we was here.'

'He'll know somebody was here,' I said. 'He won't be able to prove it was us.'

'OK,' Jerry said. 'You're the boss.'

We found some brown envelopes, stuffed them full of photos and negatives, then went out the back door to the Caddy.

Jerry looked around as he got behind the wheel.

'I don't think anyone saw us, or the car,' I commented.

'Unless somebody came out of the clubs to get a blowjob behind the building.'

I looked over at the parking lots of both clubs as we pulled out. Only a few cars, probably belonging to employees.

'I think we're in the clear,' I said, with more confidence than I felt.

'Don't worry, Mr G.,' Jerry said. 'Even if somebody saw the car we can just say we were lookin' for Irwin.'

'For over an hour?'

Jerry shrugged. 'So we decided to wait a while to see if he came home.'

'That sounds plausible.'

'It's all plausible,' Jerry said, 'just as long as when you lie, you stick to it.'

FIFTEEN

I walked into Clipper's just before six. I wondered why Irwin had picked this place. One of the strip clubs near his house might have been better for him.

I saw him first, didn't spot Danny right away, but then saw him sitting at the very end of the bar. Beyond him I could see the foyer with pay phones, and restrooms. I don't even know how I missed him. He was wearing a Hawaiian shirt, with vivid yellows, oranges and reds. But I figured he must know what he was doing, because I *did* miss him, at first.

Clipper's was a typical neighborhood joint, the same as in Brooklyn, LA, or Vegas. A worn bar, chafed wooden floors, the smell of booze, smoke and sweat. The locals would all turn whenever the door opened, greet regulars or stare at strangers for a few moments before turning back to their drinks.

Danny saw me, played it so relaxed he almost looked sleepy.

Irwin spotted me and jerked his head. He got up from the bar with a beer and walked to a booth. I got a beer from the bartender, and joined him. His clothes were still glaring. I mean, who *ever* wears white shoes? Except Pat Boone.

'I put this on your tab,' I told him, sitting.

'Yeah, yeah,' he said, sourly. He was wearing a short-sleeved, button-down shirt, and I could smell that he didn't use deodorant. It was hot, but it was more sweat from nerves than from heat.

'You got something for me?' I asked.

He looked around the place, then raised his hand. The bartender came out from behind the bar carrying a brown envelope that looked like it had been used as a coaster.

Irwin put the envelope on the table and slid it across to me.

'This is what you want,' he said.

I pushed my beer aside and opened the envelope. We were out of sight in the booth so I pulled the contents out. Photos and negatives. I put the negatives back into the envelope. The photos were all eight by tens of a young Abby Dalton. They were cheesecake, mostly bathing-suit shots, all one piece, but revealing. I stuffed them back into the envelope, pushed it aside and grabbed my beer.

'Not what I wanted, Barney,' I said.

'Whataya mean?' he asked. 'Those are the pictures I got of the kid.'

'None of these are nudes.'

'I don't do—'

'You forget what you were doing when we walked in on you yesterday?' I asked.

'That was – I didn't used to do that back then,' he said. 'Things is tough, so I'm doin' it now.'

'I don't buy it,' I said. 'You expect me to believe you had a dish like Abby Dalton in front of your lens and you didn't try to get her naked?'

'I didn't say I didn't try,' he said. 'I tried like hell, but she wouldn't go for it. She had too much class.'

Abby had all but admitted to me that there were nude photos. A teenager anxious for fame can be forgiven for a lapse in judgment, no matter how classy she actually was.

'Barney—'

'I'm tellin' ya,' he said, spreading his hands, 'I got no nudes of her. If I did I'd sell 'em to ya, and not cheap.'

If he had them, they were well hidden, but for Abby's benefit I couldn't take his word for it. I was probably going to have to let Jerry squeeze him.

'All right,' I put my hand on the envelope, 'I'll give you a thousand dollars for these.'

'You gotta be kiddin' me,' he said, scoffing. 'These shots are worth more than a thousand bucks if I wanna shop 'em around.'

'Then why haven't you shopped them?'

'I was waitin'.'

'For what?'

'I figured maybe the kid would become a movie star,' he said. 'They'd be worth more then.'

'Fifteen hundred,' I said.

Irwin smiled then.

'She wants 'em, huh?' he asked. 'She told you to buy 'em, even if they weren't nudies.'

I didn't answer.

'Ten grand,' he said. 'Take it or leave it.'

I thought I could get him down to the five she gave me, and was still convinced he had nudes. If I was going to give Jerry his chance to squeeze Irwin, this was it.

'OK,' I said.

'You got it with you?' His eyes glittered.

'No, she didn't give me that much.'

'How much did she give you?'

'Never mind,' I said. 'You want ten grand, I'll get you ten grand.'

'When?'

'Tomorrow.'

'Meet me here.'

'I don't like it here,' I said, looking around.

'Why not?' he asked. 'What's wrong with this place?'

'The beer sucks.' He looked at my mug, which I hadn't even lifted yet. 'I'll call you at your studio tomorrow and tell you where.'

'Oh, no,' he said, 'I pick the place.'

'If you want ten grand,' I said, 'then I pick it.'

He thought about that a moment, then reached out, put his hand on the envelope and slid it back to his side of the table.

'Yeah, OK, call me. But when we meet, you better have the dough with you.'

'I'll have it.'

'Ten thousand.'

'That's what we just said.'

'OK,' he said, sliding out of the booth. 'Call me, or these might find a new home.' He fanned himself with the envelope.

'Barney,' I said, 'don't make me regret being nice to you.'

SIXTEEN

Outside of Clipper's, I looked for Jerry, but if he was there he was better at blending in than Danny was.

Speak of the devil, Danny came walking out of the bar. I headed for my car, got behind the wheel and waited for him to join me.

'That's a great disguise,' I said, when he slid into the passenger seat. 'Why didn't you shoot off some flares, while you were at it?'

'See,' he said, 'this is why I'm the pro and you're the pit boss. When people see a shirt like this, they rarely look at your face. Admit it, when you walked in you didn't see me right away.'

'Never mind that,' I said. 'He didn't have the right photos.'

'I noticed you let him keep the envelope.'

'We made a deal for ten grand,' I said. 'I'm supposed to meet with him tomorrow.'

'Where?'

'I haven't decided,' I said. 'Someplace . . . quiet.'

'Quiet?'

'Yeah, I'm going to have Jerry with me,' I said. 'I think I might let him ask Irwin about the photos one more time.'

'Ask?'

'Ask.'

'Ah,' Danny said, 'someplace quiet.'

'Yes.'

'Maybe I can come up with something. You think Irwin will show?'

'He will if he wants his ten grand.'

'Where is the big guy?' Danny asked. 'I know he wouldn't let you come here alone.'

'He's around here somewhere,' I said, 'probably not wearing an ugly Hawaiian shirt.'

'Ugly? Penny said this shirt had character.'

'I think she meant it makes you look like a character.'

'Ha-ha.' He opened the car door. 'My heap is around the corner. If you need me to do anything else, let me know.'

'Thanks, Danny,' I said. 'I will.'

I watched him walk down the street until he turned the corner. I was about to start the car when Jerry appeared at my elbow.

'Shove over, Mr G.,' he said. 'I'll drive.'

Jerry said he wanted barbecue so I took him to a place I knew just a few blocks away.

'I discovered ribs last year,' he said, working on the first of two racks. 'I had a job makin' a pick-up from this Texan who thought he was gonna come to New York and score big. Well, he lost and introduced me to ribs just before I broke his arm and collected the debt.'

I picked up a rib from my half rack and gnawed on it.

'I mean, I knew what ribs was from, you know, Chinese food, but I was pretty much a steak, burger and hot dog guy until Bubba offered me some ribs.'

'Chinese ribs are pork,' I said. 'These are beef.'

'Well, that explains it then.'

'So this guy Bubba, he offered you ribs not to hurt him?'

'No, he pretty much knew I was gonna hurt him,' Jerry said. 'He was just bein' polite. When I found him he was eatin', so he offered me some.'

'And you broke his arm, anyway?'

'I was supposed to break his legs, but he was a nice guy, and he wanted to leave town so . . .' He shrugged, 'I figured I'd let him walk.'

'OK.' I dropped the last bone on to my plate.

'How did it go in the bar?'

I told him about the deal I'd made with Irwin for Abby's pictures.

'Ten grand?' Jerry said. 'You're gonna give that asshole ten large?'

'No,' I said, 'I just told him that so he'd meet us somewhere.'

'Us?'

'Yeah, us. I'm going to give you your shot at Mr Irwin.'

'I get to squeeze him?'

'Yeah,' I said, 'but that doesn't mean you get to break anything. At least, not till I say so.'

'Yeah, well, your call, Mr G.'

I started working on my fries. Jerry had dumped about half a bottle of ketchup and a pound of salt on his.

'He didn't show you any naked stuff?' he asked.

'No, just cheesecake. I think he's holding the nudes back. If he is, you're going to squeeze them out of him.'

'Yeah, I am,' Jerry said, with a barbecue-sauce-smeared grin.

SEVENTEEN

10.31 a.m., November 22, 1963

Even before I entered the lobby of the Sands I knew something was wrong. I had eaten my breakfast that day without benefit of the TV or radio, and driven directly to the casino. I still needed to work out where Jerry and I would meet Barney Irwin in order to squeeze the Abby Dalton photos out of him. We would need someplace quiet, just in case it became necessary for Jerry to break something.

As I entered the lobby, though, the climate was one of panic. People were running across the lobby, panicked, toward no apparent destination. One of the girls behind the counter was crying, and over by the pay phone a man was consoling another weeping woman. I looked around, expecting to see the cause of these reactions, but nothing was immediately evident. I scanned what was becoming a crowd in the lobby, looking for an employee I could ask, but finally had to walk to the front desk.

The hysterical girl was the same one who had given me Barney Irwin's message. I still hadn't found out her name.

'What's going on?' I asked her.

'You don't know? Oh, Mr Gianelli – Eddie, it's terrible.'

'What is?'

'The President,' she said. 'Somebody shot the President.'

'The President.' Just for a moment I thought, President of what? 'Wait . . . you mean . . . JFK?'

She nodded, held a handkerchief to her nose and began to sob.

I knew I'd get nothing else coherent out of her, so I made for the elevators, figured I'd go somewhere I knew there'd be a television.

When I got to Entratter's office I found his girl at her desk, in much the same condition as the girl at the front desk. She even neglected to sneer at me.

I entered Jack's office, found him standing in front of a large color TV in his wall. Color TV's were still not in everyone's home at that time, but the appearance of *The Wonderful World of Disney* as a weekly series in 1961 sure sent a lot of people scurrying for them.

'What's goin' on?' I asked.

He looked at me over his shoulder, then back at the TV. He was standing with his back straight, his arms folded.

'No word yet on his condition,' he said. 'We just know he was shot while in his motorcade.'

'In the car? What about the first lady?'

'Nobody said anything about her.'

I joined him in front of the TV.

'Jesus,' I said.

'Yeah.'

'It's a madhouse downstairs.'

'Yeah.'

'I didn't hear anything until I walked in.'

'It's all over the TV and radio.'

'I didn't turn either of them on this morning.'

It was all very surreal, the panic in the lobby, and the coverage on the TV. The usually stolid Walter Cronkite appeared shaken up. Cronkite was like everybody's uncle. To see him upset just added to the unsettling feeling of it all.

We stood side by side for quite a while, just watching the reports. After the fact that Kennedy had been shot it was all supposition, but a lot of people were doing the supposing.

After a few minutes I asked, 'Do we know where Frank is?'

Entratter let out a breath, as if he'd been holding it for a long time. 'I think he's home, in Palm Springs.'

'He must be taking this hard.'

From the outer office we could hear the sound of Jack's girl, blubbering.

'Hold on,' he said.

He walked out and I heard him tell the girl to go home, they weren't going to get much work done that day. She didn't argue. When he came back in he picked up his phone and called the hotel room service and ordered some coffee.

'You want something to eat?' he asked, before hanging up.

'See if they can send some pastries with it.'

He told them to send whatever they had in the way of pastries or donuts, then hung up and rejoined me in front of the TV.

'This is unreal,' he said.

'Yeah.'

We were still standing there when a bellman carrying a tray appeared at the door.

'Mr Entratter?'

'Just put it on the desk.'

The young man did so, then looked at the TV.

'Anything new?' he asked.

'No,' Jack told him, 'they still don't know his condition. Or they're not sayin'.'

'Thank you, sir.'

Jack nodded and the young man left.

'Why don't we sit down?' Jack suggested.

'Yeah, sure,' I said.

We went to his desk and sat. Entratter was a good host, poured coffee for both of us, removed the covering from the plate of pastries.

'Is Joey still in town?' I asked.

'Actually,' Entratter said, 'he left this morning. He probably heard the news on the plane.'

'That'll be a somber flight.'

'Maybe we should call Frank?' I asked. 'See how he's doing?'

'No,' Entratter said. 'Let's wait and see what else we can learn before we do that. He's probably making a lot of calls of his own. He's a lot more personally –' he groped for the word, finally came up with it – 'invested in this than we are.'

'I guess you're right.'

'So,' Jack said, picking up his coffee.

'So,' I said, grabbing a pastry.

At 1.33 CST time – an hour and three minutes after he was shot – President John Fitzgerald Kennedy was pronounced dead at Parkland Hospital, in Dallas, Texas.

EIGHTEEN

After Kennedy was pronounced dead we graduated from coffee to bourbon. Jack and I had our own private wake for a while, and then his phone began to ring.

'Not now,' he said into the phone half a dozen times before he finally covered the mouthpiece and said, 'I better take this one.'

'Yeah,' I said, getting up, 'I've got things to do.' I staggered a moment before righting myself.

'You OK?'

'Yeah, Jack, I'm OK.'

'You wanna go home or work?' he asked, and then didn't wait for me to respond. 'It's up to you.'

He waved and went back to his call. I returned the wave and left his office.

When I got back to the lobby little had changed, except the pace. There were still people there, crying, slack-faced, but they were moving much slower. Some of them even seemed to be sleepwalking.

The casino floor was much the same. Even where people were gambling they were doing it – both the gamblers and the dealers – with little interest. I wasn't needed there. As I was trying to make up my mind what to do I saw Jerry's cousin, Billy, shooting craps. He towered over the table, throwing the dice with enthusiasm. He either hadn't heard about the assassination, or he didn't care.

My face felt tight, my eyes gritty, and suddenly I had to get off the casino floor. I went to a house phone and called Jerry's room.

'What're you doin'?' I asked.

'Just hangin' around,' he said. 'Watchin' the reports on TV. You wanna come up?'

'Yeah,' I said, 'I'll be right there.'

Jerry had left the door ajar, so I knocked and walked in. He was sitting on the large sofa, in front of the color TV.

'I thought you didn't have a suite?' I asked, looking around.

'So did I,' he said. 'Billy was all excited, said a bellhop came up, told him we had to move, so he followed the guy here. I thought you arranged it.'

'Not me,' I said. 'It must've been Jack.'

'Well, I didn't have the heart to drag Billy outta here,' Jerry said. 'He thought I pulled some strings, and was real impressed.'

I walked over, stood next to the sofa and looked at the TV.

'Anything new?'

'Yeah,' he said, 'the Governor of Texas was in the car. He got shot, but he's alive.'

'Is he going to stay that way?'

'Don't know, yet.'

I looked over at the bar.

'You want a drink?' I asked.

'I'll take a beer.'

'Any in the frig?'

'I ain't looked.'

I checked, got him a can of Piels. I briefly considered some more bourbon, but in the end took a can of beer for myself, too.

I joined him on the leather sofa and handed him a can.

'Some shit, huh?' he asked, indicating the TV.

'Yeah.'

'He was a good man,' Jerry said. 'A good president.'

I didn't respond. I knew more about Kennedy the ladies' man than I did about Kennedy the politician. But I didn't think he handled the Bay of Pigs or the Cuban Missile Crisis the way an American president should have. The former turned out to be a fiasco, and he gave up too much in the latter. But of course we didn't learn all the details until years later.

'You don't think so?' Jerry asked.

'I've met him a time or two,' I said. 'He seemed like a good guy.'

'Mr S. thinks he's a fucking great president.'

'Yeah, I know he does.'

I could feel Jerry looking at me, but I kept my eyes on the TV. I didn't want to start talking politics with him. It wasn't something we had ever done before. And I wouldn't have been able to explain why I wasn't feeling much of what everyone else seemed to be feeling. Maybe I was in shock.

We ended up sitting there, staring at the TV, drinking beer, and before long we got around to business.

NINETEEN

'So what are we gonna do?' he asked.

I considered the question, coming as it did about three hours after JFK had been shot. Was that all the President of the United States was worth, three hours of our time? The truth was the nation would be mourning for weeks, maybe months. Even though the nation itself got back to business when Lyndon Baines Johnson had to be sworn in as the President of the United States aboard Air Force One at Love Field Airport, only two hours and eight minutes after JFK's death.

'I'm gonna call Danny, see if he's come up with someplace quiet for us to take Irwin, so we can talk to him properly.'

'Yeah, but first we got to get him to meet us,' Jerry said. 'Where's that gonna be?'

'I'm thinking one of those strip clubs on either side of his house.'

'Don't you think that'll be suspicious?' Jerry asked. 'He won't think that's a coincidence, us wanting to meet him right near his house?'

'I expect he already knows we were in his house, don't you?'

'Well, yeah,' Jerry said, 'once he sees those photos missin' he's gonna think of you right away.'

'So I might as well call him and see where we can set up a meet,' I said.

'If he still wants to do it.'

'He's going to be pissed,' I said, 'but he's also gonna want his ten grand. I'll give him a call at his studio.'

I walked to the phone. Jerry got up and lowered the volume on the TV.

The phone in the studio rang almost eight times. I started to think maybe Irwin was home watching television like everybody else, but right at the start of that eighth ring he picked up.

'Irwin Studios.'

'It's Eddie Gianelli, Barney,' I said.

'You sonofabitch!' he spat. 'You robbed my house.'

I could have pointed out that we didn't steal his house, we simply broke into it, but decided he was already pissed off enough.

'What do you mean?' I asked.

'Come on,' he said, 'I know it was you who swiped my pictures. I want 'em back!'

'We made a deal for the Abby Dalton photos, Barney,' I said. 'That's what I'm calling about. If you lost some others I don't know anything about it.'

'I didn't lose nothin',' he said. 'You stole 'em.'

'Do you want your ten grand or not?'

There was a moment of silence and then he said grudgingly, 'Yeah, I want the money.'

'All right, so let's meet.'

'Where?'

'Not Clipper's.'

'Well, I ain't lettin' you pick the place,' Irwin said.

'You been watching the TV, Barney? Anyplace we go is gonna be in an uproar. We need someplace quiet.'

'Then come here.'

'Your studio?'

'I'll put the closed sign out. There won't be nobody here.'

'No photo shoot today?'

'I had a couple, but they both canceled because of the President.' He sounded miffed that JFK had ruined his day.

'OK, what time?'

He thought a moment, then said, 'Six.'

'No earlier?'

'I said six.'

'Yeah, OK, fine. I'll be there at six.'

'Come alone,' he said, and hung up.

'When?' Jerry asked.

'Six.'

'That gives him hours to come up with some back-up,' Jerry said.

'You're right.'

'And he wants you to come alone, right?'

'Right.'

'Yeah,' Jerry said, 'I'm gonna have to pick the lock on that back door again.

'Can you do it quicker, this time?'

'Sure,' Jerry said, 'now that I done it once, I should be better.'

'OK,' I said, 'I'll go in the front and start talking up the exchange.'

'I'll come in the back door, take out his back-up, and then we can squeeze him.'

'Sounds like a plan.'

And like all plans, it just had to go off without a hitch . . .

TWENTY

We hung out in Jerry's room the rest of the day, followed the day's progress on the screen. The Governor had been shot in the back, but survived his surgery. His wife and the first lady had been unharmed. By the time we left at five thirty we had no news about who had fired the shots.

I called Danny before we left, told him we'd settled on a meeting place.

'OK,' he said, 'I've got somewhere for you to take him.' He gave me the address. 'Do you want me to meet you at the studio?'

'No, Jerry and I can handle that. We'll meet you later.'

'OK, but be careful.'

By the time we parked around the corner from Irwin's studio it was five fifty-three.

'Gimme ten minutes to get in the back door,' Jerry said, 'then go in.'

'Gotcha.'

He went down the alley that led behind Irwin's studio. I waited a full ten minutes and then walked around the corner and went in the front door. I had the money on me that Abby had given me, five grand.

I entered the studio, found it as musty and filthy as the last time. I decided not to go walking down the hall, looking for Irwin. Instead, I called out to him.

'Irwin! Where are you?'

I suddenly found myself hoping we weren't going to find a dead body. Jerry and I had found more than our share during the time we'd known each other.

'Hey, Barney.'

'Back here,' Irwin's voice called.

OK, so I *would* have to go down the hall. If Irwin did, indeed, have back-up with him I wondered if they'd be armed. Then I wondered if Jerry was armed. I hadn't asked him. Maybe I hadn't wanted to know.

I went down the hall and through the same curtained doorway. No naked girls, this time. Just Irwin, standing in the center of the room with his arms folded. He looked like he was posing.

'You got my money?' he asked.

'I've got it,' I said. 'You got the pictures?'

Instead of answering the question he said, 'Meet Wayne.'

'Wayne who?'

'Wayne me,' a voice said from behind me. A big man in his fifties came in through the same doorway I'd used. He had broad shoulders and muscular arms, but sported a hard paunch. He shopped the same place for clothes that Irwin did. Still, I would not have wanted to try to handle him alone.

'What's this?' I asked.

'Give me the dough.'

'Not till I see the pictures.'

Irwin shook his head and looked past me at Wayne. I turned, saw Wayne reach behind him and come up with a sap. I was glad it wasn't a gun.

I also saw Jerry's big forearm come through the curtain and snake around Wayne's neck. His other hand relieved the man of his weapon. The big man immediately began to fight, but he was no match for Jerry. His face started to change colors, and by the time it reached purple he passed out. Jerry lowered him to the floor.

I turned and looked at Irwin, who seemed panicked.

'H-hey—' he said.

'What was your plan, Barney? Have Wayne work me over and then take the money?'

'Naw, naw,' Irwin said.

Jerry stepped past me and approached the photographer. Irwin put both hands out in front of him and cringed.

'Hey, I got neighbors,' he said. 'They'll hear—'

'Relax, Barney,' I said. 'We're just gonna go for a little ride.'

'Huh? Where?'

Jerry reached out, settled one big paw on the back of Irwin's neck.

'You'll see,' he said.

Irwin looked down at Wayne and asked, 'Is . . . is he dead?'

'Naw, he's just asleep.'

Irwin looked at me, his eyes pleading.

'The pictures are here,' he claimed. 'I was gonna make the exchange. Wayne was just back-up.'

'Where are they?'

'There.' He pointed. I walked over to a table where a brown envelope lay. It had stains on it, which it had acquired that afternoon in Clipper's. It was the same envelope, with the same photos in it. No nudes.

'Not good enough, Barney,' I said. 'Where are the nudes?'

'How many times I gotta tell you—' he started, but Jerry tightened his hand on the back of Irwin's neck, which took away his ability to speak.

'Come on, Barney,' I said. 'We're going for a ride.'

TWENTY-ONE

Danny found us a downtown warehouse that had seen better days and had been empty for a while.

He was waiting for us when I pulled the Caddy up in front. I drove so Jerry could sit in the back with Irwin, making sure that Barney didn't try anything.

We got out and Irwin asked, 'Who's he?'

'Shut up,' Jerry said, and cuffed him on the back of the head.

Danny opened the door.

'Thanks, Danny.'

'It's all set,' he said. 'Just some chairs and a table.'

'Good enough.'

I let Jerry drag Irwin inside.

'Here's the keys,' Danny said, handing them to me. 'Lock up when you leave.'

'What's in here to steal?'

'Nothin',' Danny said. 'Just lock it, OK? I'm borrowin' the place.'

'OK, I'll lock up.'

'And I promised the owner you wouldn't leave any bodies behind.'

'That's a promise I can keep.'

'Sure you don't want me to come in with you?'

'No, Jerry can handle it,' I said.

'Keep him on a short leash, Eddie,' Danny said. 'He can do some real damage.'

'I know it,' I said. 'Don't worry.'

Danny slapped me on the shoulder. 'I won't worry. Let me know what happens.'

I slapped his back and went inside.

Jerry already had Irwin in a chair, his hands tied behind him. He was watching us with wide eyes, his face already slick with sweat. His skin had a yellow cast, because of the naked yellow bulb above him.

'What's goin' on?' he demanded.

'Barney, my friend does this for a living, so make this easy on yourself.'

'What are you talkin' about?'

'I want the nude photos of Abby Dalton.'

'I already toldja,' Irwin replied. 'I never took no nude photos.'

'I can't buy that, Barney,' I said. 'The way Abby looked back then, young and fresh? No way you'd let her get away without a few nudies. Somebody's threatening to take those photos public, and you're the only one who ever took any.'

'That's what she said?'

'That's what she said.'

He thought about it for a minute, then said, 'She's a liar.'

I stared at him for a few seconds. 'OK, Jerry. He's all yours.'

'What? No, hey, wait a minute—'

I went out the front door, closed it behind me and leaned against it. Danny had picked a good place. I couldn't hear anything that was going on inside. I checked my watch, and after five minutes I went back in.

Irwin was still in his chair, but his head was hanging down, his chin on his chest. I looked at Jerry.

'I think he's ready to deal,' he said.

I checked Irwin out, critically. It didn't seem that any of his appendages were broken.

'What'd you do to him?' I asked.

'Nothin',' Jerry said, 'I just kinda . . . asked him nicely.'

'Asked him nicely, huh?'

He nodded.

I walked over and stood in front of Irwin.

'Barney.'

He looked up at me. His eyes seemed haunted, but he didn't look like he was in pain.

'The nude photos of Abby,' I said. 'Where are they?'

'I got 'em . . . in the bank.'

'A safe deposit box?'

'Y-yes.'

'What bank?'

'The Bank of Las Vegas.'

'What branch?'

'The one on Simmons.'

'OK,' I said, 'how about we go there and get 'em tomorrow?'

'Sure,' Irwin said, 'OK.'

I turned and looked at Jerry.

'He'll be there, Mr G.'

'OK,' I said, turning back to Irwin, 'so let's meet in front of the bank at nine a.m.'

'Yeah, OK.' Irwin lowered his eyes, as if he couldn't meet mine. Whatever Jerry had done to him had made him feel . . . ashamed.

I walked behind him, untied his hands. He didn't bring them around in front until Jerry said, 'It's OK, Barney.'

He rubbed his wrists.

'Let's get you home,' I said. I went to grab his arm and help him up, but he flinched and pulled away.

'Come on, Barney,' Jerry said. 'We're just gonna drive ya home.'

Once again I drove while Jerry sat in the back with Irwin. When we got to his house they got out of the car together.

'I'll just walk him to the door,' Jerry said.

I watched as they walked, Jerry with his arm around Irwin's shoulder, Irwin looking completely crestfallen. At the door they stopped. Jerry turned Irwin to face him, spoke to him briefly, at which point Irwin nodded miserably, and went inside.

Jerry came back and asked, 'Can I drive?'

'Sure.'

I shoved over and allowed him to get into the driver's seat.

'Jerry, he seems like a completely broken man.'

'I know.'

'But . . . he's not. You didn't break anything . . . right?'

'Only his spirit, Mr G.,' Jerry said, 'only his spirit.'

TWENTY-TWO

By the time we got back to the Sands, Lee Harvey Oswald had been arrested and charged with the murders of a police officer, and the President of the United States. The images of Oswald in handcuffs were played over and over on the screen.

We went to Jerry's suite. He let me in and then said he was going to look for his cousin, Billy. First, I asked him to stash the five grand for me because I didn't want to carry it around, then I used the phone to call Abby Dalton's room.

'Isn't it horrible?' she asked me. 'I've been watching all day.'

'Yes, I know,' I said. 'It's hard to believe. Listen, Abby, I've been workin' on your problem and I think I'm gonna get those photos tomorrow.'

'From Irwin?'

'Yes, apparently he has them in a safe deposit box.'

She hesitated, then said, 'Maybe I should be flattered.'

'I'll come back here right away when I have the photos,' I said. 'You're probably anxious to leave Vegas and get home.'

'I do have to get back to work.'

'OK,' I said, 'just be patient one more day.'

'I'd be more patient if I had some company.'

'I'll come by in an hour and take you to dinner.'

'Wonderful! That will be so much better than sitting here watching the television.'

'I'm gonna bring a friend who's helpin' us,' I added. I figured Jerry would like to meet Abby.

'The private detective?'

'No, another friend. I think you'll find him . . . interesting.'

I hung up and dialed Entratter's office.

'Any word on Frank?' I asked when he answered.

'He was on the Warner Brothers lot shooting *Robin and the 7 Hoods* with the rest of the guys. I talked to Dean. He said Frank went directly to church, then called the White House.'

'Did the Kennedys talk to him?'

'He spoke with Pat Lawford.'

'Not Peter?'

'No. Pat told Frank she'd pass his condolences on to the family.'

'That must not have sat very well with him.'

'They closed down the set for the day. I don't know where Frank is now. Maybe with Dean. He seems to be the only one who can talk to Frank.'

'Frank's gonna want to go to the funeral.'

'Then he'll be disappointed,' Jack said. 'There's no way they'll let him go.'

'I guess we'll all just have to wait and see.'

'How are you doin' with that problem for Abby Dalton?' he asked.

'Should wrap it up tomorrow.'

'Well, at least that's good news. Let me know when it's all over.'

'I will. I should be in the building the rest of the night. I'm taking Abby to dinner, and then I'll go down to the floor for a while.'

'OK,' Jack said. 'See ya there.'

As I hung up, the door slammed open and Billy came stumbling into the room, followed by Jerry, who was about as livid as I'd ever seen him.

'Take it easy, Uncle Jerry!'

'What's going on?' I asked.

'This idiot,' Jerry said, pointing, 'is in to the casino for seventy grand!'

'Seventy?' I asked. 'Who okayed him for seventy grand?'

We both looked at Billy.

'I dunno,' he said, with a shrug. 'I asked for ten grand credit, then ten more—'

'And kept askin',' Jerry said. 'And he woulda still been askin' if I hadn't stopped him.'

'I'm close, Uncle Jerry,' Billy said. 'My system is gonna work.' He looked at me. 'I just need ten thousand more.'

'Shut up!' Jerry shouted, his face almost cherry red. 'You're done gambling.'

'But that's what we came here to do,' Billy complained.

'Yeah, with the money you brought with you. Nobody said you could run up a tab.'

'The guy downstairs said it was OK.'

'Who?' I asked.

'I don't know his name.'

Jerry gave me a look.

'I'll find out,' I said. 'Just keep him here.'

'Don't worry,' Jerry said. 'He ain't goin' nowhere.'

I left the suite and went down to see what idiot had given a twenty-one year old seventy grand worth of credit.

TWENTY-THREE

His name was Mike Dotelli, and he'd been in the pits exactly three months. Jack had promoted him, against my better judgment.

'Why would you ever OK that much credit to a kid?' I demanded.

'Why do you think I've got to account to you, Eddie?' Dotelli asked.

'It doesn't make any sense, Mike.'

'The kid shot ten grand on his own, Eddie,' Dotelli said. 'Said he was here celebrating his twenty-first birthday. Who are we to ruin the celebration?'

'How about you're ruining his life?' I asked.

Dotelli raised his eyebrows at me. He was young, maybe thirty-three. I didn't think he was ready for the pit, and this proved it to me. I had to wonder if this would prove it to Jack Entratter, as well?

'Eddie,' he said, 'if we started to worry about ruining people's lives we wouldn't let anybody play, at all.'

'Jesus, Mike,' I said, 'how high would you have let him go?'

'If his cousin hadn't yanked him outta here? Probably another thirty grand.'

'A hundred grand?' I asked. 'Happy fuckin' birthday.'

'Hey, the kid has a system,' Mike said. 'He'll be back.'

'Not if his cousin has anything to say about it.'

'You know these two?'

'Yeah,' I said, 'I know 'em.'

'Well, mark my words,' Mike said, 'he'll be back at the tables, if not here, then somewhere else.'

I shook my head and walked away from the asshole. My next stop was Jack Entratter.

'Eddie,' Entratter said, after a few minutes, 'you ain't askin' me to let this kid off the hook, are ya?'

'He never should have been on the hook at all, Jack,' I said. 'He came here with ten grand birthday money. When that was gone he should have been finished.'

'You wouldn't have given him any credit?'

'None.'

'Because he's Jerry's cousin?'

'Because he's a kid,' I said. 'Where's he going to get the money to pay up?'

'When has that ever been our problem?'

'It's our problem to show good judgment,' I said. 'I OK credit to people I know are going to be able to pay up. Otherwise, *I'm* gambling with the *casino's* money. And that's not my job. And it ain't Mike Dotelli's job, either.'

'All right,' Entratter said, sitting back in his chair. 'I'll have a talk with Mike but there's no way I can let the kid off the hook.'

'Just give him time to pay, Jack.'

'He'll have all the time he needs, Eddie. I'm not lookin' to break the legs attached to any of Jerry's relatives.'

'No,' I said, 'I guess not.'

'Can Jerry keep him under control from here on in?' Jack asked. 'Or maybe take him home?'

'I'll talk to him.'

'We can keep him away from our tables, but if he goes somewhere else . . .'

'I get it, Jack,' I said. 'I'll talk to Jerry, see what he wants to do.'

Jack nodded, stood up.

'Come on, I'll go down with you. I wanna walk the floor.'

'I'm gonna take Abby to dinner,' I said. 'Then I'll hit the floor.'

'Good, good.'

On the way to the elevators he said, 'I know you don't think

Dotelli was ready, Eddie, but mark my words, he'll make a good pit boss.'

'I don't doubt it, Jack,' I said, 'in a few years, maybe.'

He took the elevator down to the floor, while I took it up to Jerry's suite.

'Where's Billy?' I asked, when he let me in.

'In his room,' Jerry said. 'He's pissed I won't let him leave.'

'I'm taking Abby to dinner,' I said. 'She's going stir crazy in her room. You wanna come?'

'I'd really like to meet her,' he said, 'but Billy'll just go back downstairs. If I don't sit on 'im.'

'If he does he won't be able to play.' I told him about my talk with the pit boss, and with Entratter.

'Thanks, Mr G. I wouldn't expect Mr Entratter to let him off the hook,' Jerry said. 'And I'll sure as hell see that he makes good on the debt.'

'I know you will.'

'Hold on,' he said. 'I'll talk to the kid and then I'll come to dinner with you and Miss Dalton.'

'Good. I want her to know that you helped get her photos back.'

'Just let me scare the shit out of Billy, first,' he said.

TWENTY-FOUR

We picked Abby up at her room. Jerry acted like a shy kid when we met her, and she was very nice to him. She had put on a silk blouse, tight black skirt and heels.

'I figured we weren't going anywhere really fancy.'

'Just downstairs,' I said, 'unless you want to go somewhere else.'

'No, that's fine,' she said. 'I just wanted to get out of my room.'

'We could take in the show at the Copa Room, if you like,' I said. 'Tony Bennett.'

'No, really, that's all right,' she said. 'I don't think I'd be able to enjoy it. Let's just go and eat.'

'OK.'

We took her down to the Garden Room and over dinner she asked

Jerry a lot of questions about himself. He answered them as best he could, without really telling her what he did.

Over dessert I thought of a way to tell her how we got Irwin to part with the photos.

'We should be able to get them for you tomorrow.'

'Do you need more money?'

'No' I said, 'he should take the five grand.'

'I don't know how to thank you.' She looked at Jerry. 'Both of you.'

'Thank us tomorrow, when we hand you the photos,' I told her.

She suddenly looked troubled by something.

'Uh, Eddie . . .'

'Yes?'

'You're not going to . . . oh, never mind.'

'We're not going to what?' I asked. 'Look at the photos before we bring them to you?'

She nodded.

'I ain't gonna look at 'em at all, Miss Dalton,' Jerry said. 'And Mr G. is only gonna look to make sure they're the right ones.'

'I'm sorry,' she said. 'I didn't mean—'

'It's OK,' I said. 'Don't worry about it.'

'Jerry,' she said, 'you can call me Abby, you know.'

'No,' I said, 'he can't.'

In the end he was calling her Miss D.

We talked a bit about JFK, his presidency, and his assassination, and then we walked her back up to her room. On the way I offered one more time to take her to see Tony Bennett.

'Thanks,' she said, 'but I think I'll just turn in early. When you hand me those pictures tomorrow I'll head back to Hollywood. I need to get back to work or Joey might divorce me.'

'Hey, that's funny,' Jerry said. He looked at me. 'See, Joey's got the same name on the show—'

'I know, Jerry.'

When Abby closed the door and left us standing in the hall Jerry said, 'You wanna go inside with her, Mr G.? I can go downstairs . . .'

'No, Jerry,' I said, 'Abby and me, we don't have that kind of relationship. Let's go check on Billy.'

'OK, Mr G.'

* * *

Billy was gone.

'Goddamnit!' Jerry raged. He stormed around the suite. 'What the hell—'

'Maybe he just went downstairs.'

'I thought I scared the hell outta that boy!'

'Well,' I said, 'he's your cousin. If he's anything like you – and I mean, beyond the physical – then he doesn't scare easy.'

That seemed to mollify him a bit. He stopped pacing and stared at me.

'You might be right about that, Mr G.' He sat down heavily on the sofa. 'But where did he go?'

'If he went downstairs he's not going to be able to play,' I reminded him.

'But what if he goes somewhere else?'

'They won't give him any credit,' I said. 'What's he going to play with?'

'Oh shit!' He sprang up off the sofa and ran into one of the bedrooms. 'Crap!' he shouted, and ran back out. 'He took the five grand I stashed for you.'

'Abby's money?'

He nodded.

'If he gambles five grand and loses, somebody'll give him more on credit. And then I'll have to tell Abby something.'

'I gotta find him, Mr G.'

'Before he spends Abby's money.'

'If he does,' Jerry said, 'I'll make it good, Mr G. I'll pay her back. But I gotta find 'im.'

'OK,' I said, 'let's go.'

TWENTY-FIVE

We searched the Sands first, but there was no sign of Billy. I took Jerry to meet Mike Dotelli, for two reasons. I wanted to hear from Mike if he'd seen Billy again. And I wanted Jerry to know who had screwed with his cousin.

I waved Mike out from behind the pit.

'What now?' he asked.

'This is Jerry,' I said. 'It's his cousin you put in a seventy grand hole today.'

Jerry glowered at Dotelli, who reared back a bit.

'H-he put himself in a hole.'

'He's a kid,' Jerry said, 'You never should have okayed him. If I ever hear that you do it again, I'll come back and tear your arms off. Am I clear?'

'What? Clear?' Mike looked at me for help. 'Is he serious?'

'Dead serious,' I said.

'Jesus.' Mike looked at Jerry. 'Yeah, yeah, that's clear.'

'OK, then,' I said. 'Have you seen him again today? In the past hour, maybe?'

'Yeah,' Mike said, 'yeah, he came back down, tried to play some more.'

'Did you let him?' Jerry demanded.

'N-no, no,' Mike said. He looked at me again. 'Jack came down and read me the riot act. No more credit for kids. And he said not to let this particular kid play anymore, even with cash.'

'OK,' I said, 'so where did he go?'

'I don't know,' Mike said. 'He left, Eddie. He just . . . left.'

'Damn it!' Jerry said. 'He's gonna try another casino.'

'Don't worry, Jerry,' I said, 'don't worry. We'll find him. Come on.'

Outside we split up. I went left, to the Flamingo. Jerry went right, to the Desert Inn. Billy couldn't have gotten much further than that. With five grand he should still be sitting at a table in one of those casinos.

I entered the Flamingo and headed for the craps tables. I didn't see Billy. I spoke to a pit boss and a couple of dealers I knew, described the kid, but they hadn't seen him. I hoped Jerry was having better luck at the Desert Inn.

He was. I got there in time to see Jerry practically carrying Billy out the door by his collar. The kid was almost as big as his cousin, but I swore Billy's feet weren't touching the floor.

'. . . it easy, cuz,' Billy was saying. 'Jeez. I tol' you I was gonna give you back your money as soon as my system kicked in.'

'You asshole,' Jerry said. 'I don't care what kind of system you got, you don't steal from me!'

'It wasn't stealin',' Billy argued. 'It was borrowin'.'

'Borrowin' without permission is stealin',' Jerry said. 'Believe me, I know. And you don't borrow from family.'

Sometimes Jerry's values were skewed, but he kept to them. Breaking somebody's legs was OK if they deserved it, but he wouldn't steal without a very good reason, and he sure wouldn't steal from family.

And it must have confused him that he could put a scare into anybody but his own cousin.

When Billy saw me he tried to plead his case.

'Eddie, tell 'im,' he said. 'You know about systems.'

'What I know, Billy,' I said, 'is that they don't work. Casinos love jerks like you, who think they can beat the house.'

'Yeah, but my system's gonna work. I know it is.'

'Test it out with your own money,' Jerry said. He handed me the envelope with the five grand, which confused Billy, but we didn't explain it to him just then.

We started to walk toward the Sands, Jerry still holding on to Billy's collar, although the kid's feet were now touching the sidewalk.

'How the hell do you plan on payin' back seventy grand?' Jerry demanded.

'With my winnings!' Billy argued. 'Come on, cuz, it's gonna work. I'm gonna make us both rich. Just let me play your five G's.'

Jerry shook him by the collar, as if he was holding a wet cat.

'You're gonna go to the room and stay there, and you ain't gonna leave unless I say so.'

'Hey, I gotta eat—'

'Order room service,' Jerry said.

I was pretty sure room service was comped, since Jack had given them the suite, but I kept that to myself. Who knows what kind of food bill the kid could have piled up? After all, he was Jerry's family.

TWENTY-SIX

It had been a long day.

As I walked through the casino and hotel lobby everybody still seemed to be in shock. TVs and radios were still tuned to news channels, waiting for the latest word on the assassination.

As I drove home I was thinking about Frank, and how much he thought of JFK. I never had the same high opinion – and, in fact, was not that crazy about any of the Kennedy clan I'd had dealings with – Joe, Jack or Bobby. But I felt bad for Frank because, from his point of view, he'd lost a good friend. I would have called if I'd known where to get ahold of him. I wondered if he had returned to Palm Springs?

I stopped and picked up some takeout fried chicken. I didn't feel like sitting in a restaurant with a bunch of people who were in mourning, so I just sat in my own kitchen and had a snack alone. Then I turned in, hoping the next day would be better for all of us.

I was supposed to meet Irwin and Jerry in front of the Bank of Las Vegas branch on Simmons. I wondered if we'd made a mistake letting Irwin go. But when I pulled up in front there he was – easy to spot because he was wearing a paisley shirt – standing alongside Jerry.

And Billy.

'He showed up,' I said to Jerry.

'I knew he would.'

'What's Billy doing here?'

'I couldn't trust him,' Jerry said. 'I thought I'd show him a little bit of what I do.'

I glanced over to where Irwin and Billy were standing. Billy had an unhappy frown on his face, but obviously to Irwin it was more of a threatening look. He seemed very uncomfortable standing next to the younger, bigger man.

'What'd you tell Billy?'

'Just to look mean,' Jerry said, 'and not to talk.'

'Let's go in, before Irwin changes his mind,' I said. 'He could give us a hard time in the bank, start yelling or something.'

'He'll be fine,' Jerry said. 'Maybe I can't scare my own cousin, but this guy is scared.'

We entered the bank, approached a teller's window. Billy and I hung back, but Jerry went to the window with him. Irwin told the girl he wanted to access his box. She was pretty, and wary of him, and I had no doubt that he'd made a couple of efforts to get her to pose for him in the past. Today he was all business.

It went surprisingly well – surprising to me, anyway, but apparently not to Jerry.

Irwin was meek. He went into the safe with a man from the bank, came out with an envelope. We left the bank and, out front, standing by my car, he gave me the photos.

I stepped away from them, slid the photos part of the way out, meaning only to look at them long enough to make sure they were the right ones. But it was hard to slide them right back in when I got a look at a young, naked Abby Dalton. There were six different prints, but only two full frontal. In the others she was looking back over a shoulder, so that her perfect back and butt were in view. Further down in the envelope were the negatives.

'Mr G.?'

Jerry startled me, coming up behind me, and I shoved the photos back into the envelope.

'Yeah, OK,' I said. I looked at Irwin. 'These better be all of them.'

'He knows,' Jerry said, 'that if he ever comes back with more photos, he'll have to deal with me.'

'Yeah, yeah, right,' Irwin said. He was a changed man since I left him in the warehouse alone with Jerry.

'Mr G.?' Jerry asked. 'We gonna pay 'im?'

'Oh, right.' I took the envelope Abby had given me from my back pocket. 'This is what Abby gave me to give you. Take it and be happy.'

Irwin looked at Jerry first, and when the big guy nodded he accepted the envelope. To my shock and surprise he didn't count it. In fact, he didn't even open it.

'Zat it?' he asked. 'I mean, I'd like to get home . . . you know, see what else is on TV about the JFK thing.'

I didn't think Irwin cared a bit about JFK. He probably had a couple of babes lined up for a photo shoot. I wondered if I should use Jerry to put him out of business for good. Then again, why was it my concern? However he chose to make a living, that was up to him. As long as he left Abby alone.

'Yeah, that's it,' I said. 'Abby doesn't want to hear from you again, and I don't want to see you again. Got it?'

'Yeah, yeah,' Irwin said, looking not at me, but at Jerry. 'I got it.'

'Good,' I said, 'then go.'

I didn't know how he had gotten there, but he took off walking down the street, then turned the corner. Maybe he'd parked there.

'We good?' Jerry asked.

'Yeah, yeah,' I said, 'we're good. Might as well get back to the Sands and deliver these to Abby.'

Jerry and Billy had taken a cab to the bank, so we piled into my Caddy, Jerry behind the wheel and Billy in the back seat.

As we pulled away from the bank Billy leaned forward and said meekly, 'I'm hungry.'

I looked at Jerry, who returned the look and said, 'I could eat.'

'OK, sure.'

'The Horseshoe.'

We weren't far from there, and I knew Jerry liked their coffee shop, so I said, 'Why not?'

TWENTY-SEVEN

Jerry suggested calling 'the dick' to join us at the Horseshoe Coffee Shop. I called from a pay phone and Danny was there waiting when we got there.

'Get it done?' he asked, as we joined him in a booth.

'Done,' I said.

'Those the photos?' He jerked his chin at the envelope in my hands.

'I didn't want to trust leaving it in the car.'

There was no way one side of the booth would have accommodated both Jerry and Billy, so I got in on one side with Jerry, Billy joined Danny on the other side, and they shook hands dutifully.

'Is he the runt of the litter?' Danny asked Jerry.

'How'd you know?'

'Huh?' Billy said.

'Forget it,' I said.

'So this is a celebration breakfast?'

'Celebration second breakfast,' I said. But my first one had only been toast and coffee, so I went for eggs with the works.

Danny had steak and eggs, while the cousins demolished a couple of stacks of pancakes each.

'So?' Danny asked, halfway though.

'So what?'

'We get to see what's in the envelope?'

'Nope,' I said.

'What's in the envelope?'

'That wouldn't be right,' Jerry said.

'Just a peek,' Danny said.

'What's in the envelope?' Billy asked, again, pouring syrup on to his second stack.

'Never mind,' Jerry said. 'It just wouldn't be right.'

'You haven't seen them?' Danny asked Jerry.

'No.'

Danny looked at me.

'He wouldn't look if I gave them to him.'

'What a gentleman,' Danny said.

'What's in the damn envelope?' Billy asked.

'None of your business!' Jerry snapped.

'Jeez,' Billy said.

'What's with the cousins?' Danny asked.

'Family tensions.'

'I'd hate to be at the reunions,' Danny said.

'There,' Jerry said, 'you'd be the runt of the litter.'

The waitress came to clear the wreckage when we were done, and we all got seconds and thirds on the coffee.

'So, what's the next step?' Danny asked.

'Just get these to Abby,' I said. 'Then she's on her way back to Hollywood, and we have our lives back.'

'I guess we should all get back to our lives,' Danny said. 'I mean, after what happened yesterday.'

'Why not?' I asked. 'We get a new president an hour later. The government goes on, so should we.'

'Anybody talk to Sinatra?' Danny asked. 'See how he's handling this?'

'Entratter found out where he was when he heard,' I said. 'On the set.'

'And now?'

'I guess they closed it down, for the day at least. I don't know where he is now.'

'Mr S. is a pro,' Jerry said. 'He'll be back on the set today or tomorrow.'

'Probably,' I said.

Billy looked over at the envelope beneath my elbow and asked, 'Come on, what's in the envelope?'

Outside the Horseshoe, Danny asked, 'You guys gonna do some gambling down here?' He was looking at the cousins.

'Yes!' Billy said.

'No!' Jerry said. He grabbed his cousin by the scruff of the neck and walked him away.

'What's that about?'

'The kid got himself in the hole seventy grand.'

'Yikes. Who gave him that much credit?'

'It was a mistake,' I said.

'You?'

'No, not me. A lunkhead Entratter promoted to pit boss.'

'Has he met Jerry?'

'Yes,' I said, 'he's not gonna make that mistake again.'

'Well,' Danny said, 'at least now I understand the family tension.'

'I'll talk to you soon,' I said.

'Yeah, sure,' Danny said. 'Thanks for breakfast.'

He went to his office, which was only a few doors away, and I joined Jerry and Billy in the Caddy.

TWENTY-EIGHT

We drove back to the Sands. Jerry dragged Billy up to their suite, and I went to Abby's room. When she opened the door I held the envelope out to her.

'Oh God!' she said, grabbing it with one hand and my arm with the other. She pulled me inside.

'Make sure they're all there,' I said, 'but I think he was too scared to hold any back.'

'Scared?' she said,

'You don't want to know,' I said. 'Just check.'

She opened the envelope, slid the prints out and looked at them one by one. Then she looked further and found the negatives.

'All there?' I asked.

'Looks like it.' She slid them back in. 'Did you, uh, look at them?'

'Just took a peek to make sure it was you,' I said, lying just a little.

She hugged the envelope to her chest. She was wearing a sleeveless dress, the length of which came to mid knee. There were suitcases by the door.

'Catching a plane?' I asked.

'In two hours, I had hoped,' she said, 'so I guess so. I don't know how to thank you.'

'It was my pleasure, Abby.'

'Joey says you don't take money, but—'

I waved her off. Suddenly, she took a few steps and grabbed me in a tight hug. She smelled great and we stood that way for a few moments.

'Well,' she said, backing away, 'I guess I should head for the airport.'

'I'll have a bellman come up for your bags,' I said, 'and take care of checking you out.'

'Eddie, I see why Joey, Frank, and all the guys have such a high opinion of you.'

'Thank you, Abby,' I said. 'That means a lot.'

She kissed me goodbye. Down in the lobby I told the desk she was leaving, and had them send a bellman up. That done, I went to let Jack Entratter know that my business with Abby Dalton was done, and I'd be going back to work.

His girl still wasn't at her desk. I knocked on his open door, and he waved me in.

'What's up?'

'I got the Abby Dalton thing done.'

'Good,' he said. 'What's Jerry doin' about his kid cousin?'

'I'm not sure, but I'm guessing he's gonna take him home and try to keep him out of trouble.'

'And are we gonna get paid?'

'Don't worry, Jack,' I said. 'You'll get paid.'

'Cousin Jerry's got that kind of cash?'

'I don't know what kind of cash Jerry's got, but I know he'll bend over backwards to make sure the Sands gets its dough.'

'I hope you're right, Eddie.'

'When have I ever lied to you, Jack?'

'I ain't talkin' about lyin', kid,' Entratter said. 'I'm just talkin' about bein' wrong.'

'Well, I'm not wrong about this.'

'OK, then,' he said. 'I'll take your word for it.'

I looked over at his TV, which was dark.

'I'm tired of seein' all the reports,' he said. 'Had to shut the damn thing off.'

'Can't blame you for that,' I said. 'I'm going to work, Jack. Gonna take an extra shift this afternoon, and then do my regular tonight.'

'Go ahead, then,' he said. 'I've got work of my own to do.'

TWENTY-NINE

The country had withstood another shock when, two days after JFK was killed by Lee Harvey Oswald, Oswald was shot by a saloonkeeper named Jack Ruby. Ruby was somebody the people in my world – Entratter, Skinny D'Amato, Momo Giancana, even Frank – knew. Suddenly, speculation that the mob was behind the assassination sprang up. But so far it couldn't be proven. It appeared Oswald acted alone, and then Ruby acted alone. Of course, none of us on the outside were privy to the inner workings of the case. And, as the years went by, conspiracy theories would multiply.

But when I woke that morning I had been back to work a week, Jerry had dragged Billy back to Brooklyn and put him to work paying his debt, Frank had gone back to work, JFK had been buried, the image of John John saluting his father's motorcade was forever burned into the psyche of us all, and the country had gone back to whatever they had been doing before that day in Dallas.

And somebody was slamming their fist on my front door.

'All right!' I yelled, stumbling out of bed in my underwear. If they wanted me so bad they'd have to accept me as I was. I secretly hoped it would be some Jehovah's Witnesses I could shock.

But when I opened the door I was the one who was shocked. Detective Hargrove of the Las Vegas PD was standing there with a couple of cops in uniform.

'Get dressed,' he said. 'You're comin' with us.'

'What the hell—'

'Get dressed, Eddie.'

'Hargrove, what's this abou—'

'These two men are ready, willing and able to dress you, if you force the issue.'

'I'm not forcing anything,' I said, 'I'm just trying to find out—'

'You'll find out what's goin' on when we get downtown, Eddie,' Hargrove said. 'Now don't make me tell you again. Get dressed!'

'OK, OK,' I said, 'Jeez, relax.'

I started to close the door, but he blocked it with his hand.

'We'll come inside and wait for you, if you don't mind.'

'Like I have a choice?'

Before long I was in an interview room with a cardboard cup of coffee that actually tasted like cardboard.

They let me stew for forty minutes before Hargrove came in, carrying a folder. He sat across from me, opened the folder and pushed it across to me. I stared down at the picture of a dead guy.

'You know him?'

'No.'

'You didn't even think about it.'

'I don't have to,' I said. 'I don't know him.'

'You don't know him.'

'No.'

'Have you ever seen him?'

I hesitated, then looked again.

'Maybe. He looks kinda familiar.'

'From where?'

'I don't know. Maybe the casino?'

He took the folder back.

'Who killed him?' I asked.

'What makes you think he's been killed?'

'Why else would you be involved?' I asked. 'Unless you've been moved from Homicide?'

'No,' he said. 'And that's what I'm tryin' to find out, who killed him.'

'What makes you think I'd know?'

'We got a tip.'

'Anonymous?'

'What else?'

'And the tipster said I killed him?'

'Not exactly,' Hargrove said. 'They just said we should look into you.'

'Look into me?' I asked. 'That's it. And for that you woke me up and dragged me down here?'

'I suppose I should've called you and made an appointment?'

'You could've called me, yeah,' I said. 'I would've come down here if you asked me to.'

'Because you're such a good citizen.'

Because I worked at the Sands for Jack Entratter, and did favors for Frank Sinatra, Hargrove has always had it in his head that I was connected. And maybe I was, but not in the way he thought.

'OK,' he said, 'get out of here.'

'That's it?'

'That's it.'

He looked miserable. Apparently, he had high hopes that I was involved. But even if I was, did he think I'd admit it?

I left the building, walked a few blocks, then caught a cab and had it take me back to my house. I went inside, took a shower and dressed in fresh, clean jeans and a T-shirt. Then I grabbed my windbreaker and keys and left again. I needed some breakfast, and some time to think.

I drove to a nearby diner, ordered bacon and eggs and settled in with a cup of coffee to figure out what the hell was going on.

I had thought the business with Barney Irwin was over and done when we got Abby's photos back from him. But now, apparently, it had come back, and since Abby and Jerry had gone back home, I was the only one left to deal with it.

When Hargrove pushed that photo across the table at me, my first instinct was to lie and say I'd never seen the man before. But the fact was, I did know him. It had been a photo of Wayne, the man who had been in the studio with Barney Irwin that day when Jerry and I grabbed him and took him to that warehouse.

Jerry had choked Wayne out that day, but since then somebody had killed him – and somebody had tried to put the blame on me.

THIRTY

After breakfast I drove to Barney Irwin's studio and found it closed up. I put my nose against the window, trying to see inside. It looked as I remembered it, dusty and worn out. The windows were thick with grime. It had only been a week, but the place seemed as if it had been deserted for years.

I tried the door, found it locked tight. I went around the back, found that door locked, too. I didn't have Jerry's ability to pick a lock, but I knew somebody who did.

I found a pay phone on the street and called Danny Bardini's office.

I was sitting in my Caddy in front of Irwin Studios when Danny arrived. He stopped his heap behind me and got out.

'What's up?' he asked.

'I need to get inside.'

'Why?'

I explained about Irwin's friend, Wayne, who I had only met once.

'So you think Irwin killed him and is tryin' to sic the cops on you?'

'I don't know if he killed Wayne,' I said. 'I'm not sure he has the balls for that. But he has the balls to call the cops and send 'em looking for me.'

'So now you're lookin' for him.'

'I just want to ask him.'

'I thought Jerry said the guy wouldn't be back.'

'Irwin's afraid of Jerry,' I said. 'He's not afraid of me.'

'OK,' Danny said, 'so you want me to pick a lock? In broad daylight?'

'There's a back door,' I said. 'Come on.'

Danny picked the back door lock – a lot quicker than Jerry had – and we entered.

'Let's split up,' I said. 'I want to find anything that might tell us where he is.'

'Right.'

We went through the place, every drawer and closet and corner, and didn't find a thing. Danny finally joined me back in Irwin's office. I was standing behind the desk, going through his phone book.

'What'd you find?' I asked.

'Nothin' but a lot of dirt,' Danny said. 'I need a shower after this. What about you?'

'No, nothing,' I said. 'I'll take this phone book with me. Maybe somebody in here knows where he is.'

'Nothin' in the drawers?'

'No, noth . . . Wait a minute.' I started going through the pockets of my windbreaker.

'What is it?'

'Last time I was here, with Jerry,' I said, 'I found something – here it is.'

I took the slip of paper I had found, with some names on it, out of my pocket.

'What's that?'

'I don't know,' I said. 'Here.'

I handed it to Danny to read.

Nov. 22.
Sinatra.
Keenan & Amsler.
Barry.
Johnny.
Canoga Park.

'What's this supposed to mean?' he asked.

'I don't know,' I said, 'but it's got November twenty-second on it. And Frank's name.'

'So what? Do you know who Keenan and Amsler are?'

'No, never heard of 'em.'

'And Johnny?'

I shrugged.

Danny handed it back.

'That makes as much sense as if you'd found a grocery list in his desk.'

I stuffed the paper back in my jacket pocket and said, 'Yeah, maybe. We better get out of here.'

I took the phone book and we left, locking the back door behind us.

'What now?' he asked, as we walked down the alley. 'You wanna check out his house?'

'Might as well.'

When we got to our cars he said, 'You lead the way.'

'Gotcha!'

We convoyed our way to Irwin's house.

THIRTY-ONE

'Two strip clubs,' Danny said, shaking his head as we got out of our cars.

'Yup.'

'This house has been here a while,' Danny said as we made our way up the walk. 'Strip clubs probably got built up around it.'

We got to the front door and stopped, looked both ways. It was early, and the strip club parking lots were empty.

'Let's go to the back,' I said, 'just to be on the safe side.' I led the way.

There was no car front or back. This time Danny didn't have to pick the lock. He used a piece of plastic to simply slip it.

The inside of the house was musty. Danny sniffed the air.

'Days,' he said. 'Nobody's been here for days.'

Just to be sure, we did a search of the house. Everything was covered with a layer of dust.

'It looks to me like your boy went underground after he left you and Jerry. Maybe he didn't want Jerry to find him, again.'

We went to the bedroom.

'There are clothes here, but not enough,' Danny said. 'And no suitcase.'

'So he packed and left.'

'Looks like. There's no money around, no bank books. Everybody leaves extra cash in the house.'

'In the cookie jar?'

We went to the kitchen and looked. Nothing.

'Now what?' Danny asked.

'His bank,' I said.

'You know where he banks?'

'I know where he has a safety deposit box.'

'Might not be the same one where he has an account, though. And even if he does, why would they tell us anything?'

'We just need to know if the account's been closed.'

He thought a minute.

'I suppose I could run some kind of scam on a teller—'

'Wait,' I said. 'When we were there to pick up the pictures he went to a teller, a pretty girl. She didn't like him.'

'That's it, then,' Danny said. 'All I have to do is play her. You just have to point her out.'

'Let's go, then.'

I went into the bank with him just long enough to point out the girl, then I went outside to wait.

'OK,' he said, when he came out. 'He closed his account.'

'She just told you that?'

'I turned on the charm,' he said, with a grin. 'Showed her the ol' profile.'

'And?'

'And she hates Irwin,' Danny said. 'He was a pig, and gave her the creeps. Was always saying he wanted to take her picture. She's smart, she knew what that meant.'

'But not too smart to fall for your line?'

'What line? I told her who I was, that I was looking for him for a client.'

'The truth worked?'

'The truth works a lot,' he said, with a smile. 'It's just not always as much fun.'

'So he closed his office, left his house, closed out his bank account. Any idea how much he had in there?'

'No. She said she couldn't tell me that. I let her have one.'

'Yeah, OK. You think he left town?'

'Maybe,' he said. 'If he killed Wayne, he better have left town. If he had Wayne killed, he may still be around. If he's looking to fuck you up, he might want to stay around to watch.'

'He's the only one who would have called the cops on me,' I said. 'It's got to be him.'

'Then he's around,' Danny said. 'And since it didn't work, he may try something else.'

'I'll be on the lookout.'

'Call me if you need anything,' he said.

'I will.'

'And I'll keep my ears open. Maybe I can locate Irwin.'

'I'd appreciate it.'

'Let's get the hell out of here,' he said.

We shook hands at the cars, and drove our separate ways.

THIRTY-TWO

I went home, but didn't want to be there if the cops, or somebody else, came looking, so I dressed for work – dark suit, light blue shirt, black tie – and then drove to the Sands.

I wasn't scheduled for a shift till that night, but that was OK. I still had some telephone work to do. I took the elevator to the business offices floor and claimed an empty desk. I dialed Jerry's home number, hoping he wasn't out breaking somebody's arms or legs.

'Hey, Mr G.,' he said, when he heard my voice. 'You ain't callin' to check on Billy's IOU, are ya?'

'Not my job, Jerry,' I assured him. 'How's the kid doing?'

'He went to Atlantic City, Mr G., and lost some more dough on that system of his.'

'System players, Jerry,' I said. 'There's not much you can do about it.'

'Really? Lately I been thinkin' I been bustin' the wrong heads. What's goin' on there?'

'Well, I'll tell you . . .' And I did. Jerry remembered Detective

Hargrove very well, and listened in silence until I finished my tale.

'I agree with the dick, Mr G.,' he said. 'Irwin is still around.'

'What about you?' I asked. 'Anything happening there? I'm thinking he might've sent somebody to Brooklyn to jam you up.'

'Nope, nothin' here,' he said. 'I ain't bein' watched, either. I'd know.'

'OK, so he's still afraid of you.'

'I guess,' Jerry said, 'I shoulda done somethin' before I left to scare him off ya. Sorry, Mr G.'

'Not your fault, Jerry,' I said. 'I'm just glad you're OK.'

'So what are you gonna do?'

'Watch my ass,' I said, 'and see if I can find Irwin before he tries anything else.'

'You gotta be careful, Mr G.,' he said. 'That Irwin guy ain't got the balls for murder, but it don't take balls to hire it done.'

'That's what I figure, too,' I said.

'Make sure Bardini watches your back.'

'He will.'

'Call me if ya need somethin'.'

'You're the first one on my list, Jerry.'

I hung up, thought about going into Entratter's office, but decided instead to simply call him.

'What can I do for you, Eddie?'

'You got a number for Frank, Jack?' I asked. 'I assume he's still shooting?'

'Yeah, they'll be at it for a while,' Entratter said. 'Sure, kid, give 'im a call. He'll like hearin' from you.'

He gave me the number, which I wrote down. I broke the connection, and then dialed. It was the Biltmore Hotel, and I had to leave a message, which I did. Just my name and number. It had been a week since JFK's assassination, and I figured if I didn't check in with Frank now it'd look bad for me. Besides, I genuinely wanted to see if he was OK.

I had a small phone book of my own that I'd started carrying, ever since I'd needed to call Dino while Jerry and I were in LA. Dean wouldn't be staying in a hotel while shooting *Robin and the 7 Hoods*, because he always lived in Beverly Hills. I ended up talking to his wife, Jeannie, who I had met several times.

'He's on the set, Eddie,' she said. 'He won't be back till this evening. Can I give him a message?'

'I was gonna check in with him about how Frank was doing with this JFK thing. I left a message for Frank at his hotel, but thought I might get a more truthful response from Dean.'

'Frank took it hard, Eddie, especially since they wouldn't let him attend the funeral. Plus, it was Peter's wife who told him he couldn't come.'

Ouch, I thought. That was adding insult to injury. Peter was still number one on Frank's shit list since the fiasco with JFK staying at Bing's house instead of Frank's. The odd thing was, Frank had no anger toward Bing, and actually had Bing replace Peter on the *7 Hoods* shoot.

'I'll try Dean again later, Jeannie,' I said. 'I'll be working tonight.'

'OK, Eddie. Come and see us some time, huh?'

'You bet.' I'd have to go to Beverly Hills to see her, because she rarely accompanied her husband to Las Vegas.

I hung up, tapped the phone with my index finger, then made several more calls before standing up and leaving the room. I'd dropped Irwin's name on a few of my local contacts, in the hopes that one of them might spot him, or hear something. At the moment there was nothing else I could do. Eventually, I might go and talk to Entratter. Maybe he'd be able to help locate Irwin through some of his contacts, if mine didn't pan out. My people were on the street, though, vendors, doormen, valets, the locals who saw everything that happened in Vegas, heard everything. If anybody was going to help me locate Irwin, it would be one of them, or Danny.

THIRTY-THREE

During the night – a busy one, since it was a Friday – Entratter came down to the casino floor and showed up at my pit.

'What kind of a night are we havin'?' he asked, as I came around to greet him.

'Good,' I said. 'A couple of high rollers came in for the weekend.'

'Why didn't I know about 'em?' he asked, with a frown.

'It was a spur of the moment thing,' I said. 'Don't worry, I made sure they're staying here. I got them two suites.'

'Good work. Anything going on with you?'

'Why do you ask?'

'Because, Eddie,' he said, giving me a look, 'somethin's always goin' on with you.'

'Well, now that you ask . . . let's get a drink.'

We went to the Silver Queen lounge and sat at the bar, eyeing the Allan Stewart mural that ran the length of the wall behind it. It illustrated the history of Vegas from Gold Rush to A-bomb.

It was quiet in the lounge. About an hour ago Jack Jones had wrapped up a set, and while half of that crowd was still there, they were well-behaved, sharp-dressed men with their elegant ladies. That was the kind of crowd Mr Jones attracted.

When we had a beer each I said, 'I got a visit from Detective Hargrove. He hauled me in for questioning this morning.'

'What did you do now?' Entratter asked. 'Oh, wait. It's more likely something you and Jerry did while he was here, right?'

'It ain't even our fault,' I said. I told him about going to see Irwin – without telling him exactly why – and how he had some cheap muscle named Wayne there who Jerry had choked out fairly easily.

'He killed him?'

'No,' I said, 'we left him sleeping on the floor.'

'And?'

'Now, a week later, he turns up dead.'

'What's that got to do with you?'

'Hargrove got an anonymous call and somebody dropped my name in his ear.'

'This Irwin guy?'

'That's what I figured.'

'You go and see him?'

'He's gone to ground,' I said. 'His studio and home are empty.'

Entratter took a pad and pen from inside his jacket.

'Gimme his particulars.'

I told him Irwin's full name, described him, and both his addresses.

'I'll see what I can find out.' He stashed the pad away. 'You put out the word?'

'Yeah, and Danny's keeping his ears open.'

'That big Jew ain't here, is he?'

'No,' I said, 'Jerry's in Brooklyn.'

'Good. We don't need him tearin' through this town.'

'Jerry's got more finesse than you'd think, Jack,' I said.

'Yeah, sure,' he said, taking a hit of his beer, then shoving it aside. 'I'll catch up with you later.'

I grabbed my beer and gave it a little more attention than he'd given his. A cute waitress came over and flashed me a smile. She was new, and reminded me that I still hadn't learned the name of the new girl behind the desk in the hotel.

So many pretty girls, so little time.

THIRTY-FOUR

Barney Irwin disappeared.

Into the first week of December the photographer still had not reappeared. With all the contacts we had – mine, Danny's and Jack Entratter's – we still received no word of him being spotted anywhere in Vegas.

But, on the bright side, nobody had tried to frame me for murder again. Hargrove had come around one more time, but he'd done so a little more politely, possibly because Jack Entratter had sent him word not to harass me. He'd simply asked a few questions about Wayne and Barney Irwin, and then I didn't see him again.

I had one conversation with Frank during that time, and he told me he was doing fine. Then I talked with Dino, who said that Frank was still depressed over JFK, but that it wasn't showing in his work. But Frank was a pro. He'd never let his private life interfere with his professional one.

The morning of December 9th I was home in bed when the phone rang. At least it wasn't someone banging on my door. I rolled over and grabbed the handset on the fifth ring.

'Yeah, what?'

'Eddie? You awake?'

'Not really,' I said. 'Whozit?'

'Eddie, goddamnit, wake up! It's Frank.'

'Frank?' I sat up in bed. 'What's going on, Frank? You in town?'

'No, I'm in Reno,' he said. 'I need you to come here.'

'Why? What's going on?'

'I'll tell you when you get here,' Frank said. 'Don't tell anybody you're coming.'

'Frank—'

'Goddamnit, Eddie!' he said, cutting me off. 'No more questions! I need you here now! Yes or no?'

'Sure, Frank,' I said. 'Where are you? Cal-Neva?'

'No,' he said, 'I'm at the Mapes Hotel. Just ask for me at the desk. Pack a bag.'

'The Mapes—' I caught myself before I asked another question. 'OK, Frank. I'll be there as soon as I can get a flight.'

'Take a 'copter,' Frank said. 'It's waiting for you at McCarron.'

'You cleared this with Jack, Fra—?' I started to ask, but he hung up.

I hung up, wondering if I should call Jack Entratter and check. I decided that if the helicopter was waiting for me when I got there, it meant Entratter had okayed it.

I got dressed and drove to the airport.

There was a car waiting for me when we landed in Reno. All the driver said was that his name was Walter. He took my bag and tossed it in the trunk, then drove me right to the Mapes.

The Mapes Casino and Hotel was located on Virginia and E. To get there from the airport we drove past the Flamingo, The Sahara, and the five showgirls standing on the marquee over the doors to the Primadonna casino. At night all five ladies lit up. Just south of the Primadonna was the Horseshoe, across the street from Harrah's.

The Mapes had a twelve-story hotel and, according to their marquee, Milton Berle was playing.

I asked for Frank at the desk. They told me he was on the eleventh floor. When I asked what room, they just said to go up to the eleventh floor. On the twelfth floor was their restaurant, The Sky Room.

Still wondering what the fuck was going on, still shaking off the cobwebs, I took the elevator up. When the doors opened I stepped out, and immediately got grabbed on both sides.

'Hey!'

'We just have to frisk you, Mr Gianelli,' one man said.

'Frisk me for what?'

'Just a precaution.'

They put me against the wall, face first, started patting me down. One lifted my wallet, took a look at my license, and put it back.

'While you're at it you want to show me some ID?' I asked. In my mind it was a toss-up – cops, or hoods.

They finished patting me down, turned me around and put their IDs in my face. FBI.

'What the hell—' I said.

'This way.'

They walked ahead of me, which was encouraging. That meant I was following them of my own free will, not being 'taken' by force.

They stopped at a door with no number on it, knocked and opened it.

'He's here,' one said.

'Go on in,' the other one said.

I entered the room, the two FBI agents closed it from the outside.

The room was full of men. When I entered they spread out a bit, revealing Frank in their midst. He was sitting by the window, next to a table with a phone on it. He was holding something in his hands, clenching and unclenching. I realized it was a roll of dimes.

There were five other men in the room with us. One of them stepped forward and put out his hand.

'I'm Jim Mahoney, Eddie, Frank's publicist.'

In fact, he was Frank's new publicist, replacing Chuck Moses, who I knew.

'This man is Bill Raggio, District Attorney of Washoe County, Nevada; that's Frank's lawyer, Mickey Rudin. These two gents, and the two outside, are FBI agents.'

'Hello, Frank,' I said.

'Hey, Eddie,' Frank said, without taking his eyes off the phone. 'Thanks for coming.'

'You wanna tell me what this is about?'

Frank tore his eyes away from the phone to look at me.

'You guys wanna step outside, let me talk to Eddie?' he asked.

'Mr Sinatra—' Raggio started.

'Frank, listen—' Rudin said.

'I just need a few minutes to talk to my friend!' Frank shouted. 'Get the fuck out!'

One by one the men filed out. Rudin went last, pulling the door closed.

Frank turned to me, a haunted look in his eyes. I'd never seen him so distraught.

'They took my boy, Eddie,' he said. 'They took Frankie.'

THIRTY-FIVE

'Frank,' I said, because I didn't know what else to say.

'I went back to Palm Springs for the weekend and got the call there. They took him from Harrah's in Tahoe last night. He was performing with Tommy Dorsey.'

'What do they want?'

'They haven't said, yet. They did say they'd call me here.'

'Did they tell you not to call the police? Or the FBI?'

'No, they never said a word about that. I called Mickey, and he insisted we call the FBI.'

'So they're gonna call here and tell you how much they want,' I said. 'Frank . . . how much can you cover?'

'I'd give them a million if they give me Frankie back.'

'Can you get that much?'

'I already talked to my banker, Al Hart. He's President of City National Bank of Beverly Hills. He'll let me have whatever I need.'

'Well, you've got the FBI, your manager, and your lawyer—'

'Jilly and Jack will be here soon.'

Jilly Rizzo was one of Frank's best friends, as was Jack Entratter. It made sense they'd be there.

'OK, so with all those guys here,' I asked, 'why am I here?'

Frank stood up. He switched the roll of dimes to his left hand, and put his right on my arm.

'When they make their demand I want you to make the drop, Eddie.'

'Me? Make the pay off? But . . . why?'

'Because I trust you,' Frank said. 'You've proven to me time and again that I can trust you. You get things done.'

'Frank . . . don't you think this is somethin' the cops or FBI should handle?'

'No.' He slapped me on the arm, then flipped the dimes back to his right hand. 'It's your kind of job, Eddie.'

He sat back down by the phone.

The door opened and Mickey Rudin stuck his head in.

'They're here, Frank.'

'Bring 'em in,' Frank said.

'And the FBI?'

'No,' Frank said, 'all you guys stay out in the hall a little longer.'

Rudin nodded, backed out. The room was significantly larger with the other men out in the hall, but this was hardly the caliber of place Frank Sinatra usually stayed in. This was a weekend warrior's room, the folks who came to Reno to make a killing at the casinos during their vacation. Double bed, end table with phone, dresser, ice bucket and glasses, one cheap armchair and a TV. Not much more.

The door opened and Jack Entratter entered, followed by Jilly Rizzo. Jack filled the room with his bulk, but Jilly hardly took up any. They both rushed to Frank, who barely had time to stand before they were hugging him.

'Anythin' you want done, Frank, just say the word,' Jack told him.

'Same here, buddy,' Jilly said.

'I know I can count on you guys,' Frank said. 'It's those clowns in the hall I ain't so sure about.'

'Are we keepin' this quiet, Frank?'

'We're not lettin' it out,' Frank said, 'but it'll get out. It's too damn big not to.'

'Biggest kidnapping since the Lindbergh baby,' Jack said.

I thought about that for a minute, then figured he just might be right.

Jack looked at me, 'Thanks for comin', Eddie.'

'I figured you knew.'

'Frank asked for you, but he didn't tell me why.'

He and Jilly both looked at Frank.

'He wants me to make the pay-off,' I said.

Jack thought a moment, then said, 'Well, why not? He knows he can trust you.'

I had expected Jack to maybe get upset that Frank hadn't asked him to deliver the money, so his reaction surprised – and pleased – me.

'Do we know how much they want?' Jilly asked.

'No,' Frank said. 'They haven't made that call yet.'

'How did this happen?' Jack asked.

'We heard from Joe Foss, one of Dorsey's musicians. He was in the room with Frankie when the kidnappers knocked on the door, pretending to be from room service. They tied Foss up at gunpoint and took Frankie out. Foss got loose and called the cops. They put up road blocks right away, but they came up empty. I heard from Tino –' That was Tino Barzie, Frank's manager who was also handling Frankie – 'in Palm Springs. Then I got a call and a guy told me they had Frankie, and I was to come here and wait for their call.'

'That's it?' Jack asked.

'That's it.'

The door opened again and this time it was Bill Raggio who came in.

'Mr Sinatra, we need to talk.'

'Yeah, yeah, OK, come on in,' Frank said. He looked at all three of us and said, 'I got you rooms on this floor. These bozos will show you where.'

The bozos in question were the FBI agents. One of them told the other three to show us to our rooms, as Raggio, Rudin and Mahoney once again surrounded Frank.

Jack, Jilly and I walked down the hall with the three FBI men. We each had a room, identical to Frank's.

'Can we get room service?' Jack asked.

'Tell me what you want,' one FBI man said, 'and I'll have it brought up.'

'A bottle of bourbon, and some ice.'

'Comin' up.'

'You guys join me in my room in a few minutes,' Jack said.

Jilly and I both nodded, and went into our rooms. I had only brought one change of clothes, so I didn't bother unpacking. I went to the bathroom, ran some cold water, washed my face, then left and went to Jack's room.

THIRTY-SIX

The two FBI agents eyed me in the hall but didn't stop me from knocking on Jack's door. He opened it and let me in. I was surprised that the bottle and the ice were already there.

'Drink?' he asked.

'I could use one.'

He poured and handed me one. Jilly wasn't there, yet.

'This is insane, Eddie.'

'I know it.'

'I don't know if Frank can handle this.'

'He looks pretty rattled, but he seems OK.'

'He's right on the edge,' Jack said. 'Believe me, I know.'

There was a knock. He let Jilly in and handed him a drink. We shook hands, which we hadn't had a chance to do earlier.

'Been a while, Eddie,' he said. 'Sorry it's under these circumstances.'

'Agreed.'

'I was just tellin' Eddie how close to the edge Frank looks,' Jack said.

'You might be right,' Jilly said, 'but Frank's pretty tough.'

'Yeah, but this is Frankie,' Jack said. 'This is his kid, you know?'

'Jesus,' Jilly said, 'Nancy must be a wreck over this.'

'You think he called her?' Jack asked.

'I'm damn sure of it,' Jilly said. 'Nancy and Dolly, both.'

I knew Nancy was Frank's ex and Dolly was his mother, but I had never met either.

Jack was sitting on his bed. Jilly sat next to him. I pulled a chair over and sat down.

'To Frankie,' Jack said, lifting his glass.

'And his safe return,' Jilly said.

I raised my glass and said, 'Amen.'

'Frank called me this morning,' I explained, 'told me to get my ass here fast, but didn't tell me what it was about. You guys know more than I do. Fill me in.'

'Well, he told me Frankie got snatched, but not the particulars,' Jack said. 'I only know what he told all of us a few minutes ago.'

'Poor Frank,' Jilly said. 'He still hasn't gotten over JFK's death, and now this.'

'And the funeral snub,' Jack said. 'You'd think they could've at least let him attend the funeral. After all, he did help get JFK elected.'

'Help?' Jilly said. 'He got Kennedy elected, plain and simple.'

'I've spoken to him since the twenty-second, but he insisted he was fine.'

'That sure don't look like fine to me,' Jilly said.

'Hey, I didn't ask, Eddie,' Jack said. 'Did you agree to make the drop for Frank?'

'Well, yeah,' I said. 'I was kind of surprised, but how could I say no?'

'I don't know how much they're gonna ask for,' Jack said, 'but the Sands will stand for it. I got to tell him that.'

'I'm sure he'll appreciate it,' Jilly said.

Entratter leaned forward and filled our glasses again. We all grabbed some more ice.

'You gonna make the drop alone?' Jack asked.

'I guess . . .'

'I mean,' he went on, 'I suppose they'll want someone to make it alone, but it would probably be smart to have some back-up. Know what I mean?'

'Yeah you're probably right.'

'What about Bardini? He in town?'

I shook my head.

'He left a few days ago on a case.'

'Well,' Jack said, 'that leaves Jerry.'

I hadn't thought of that, and wondered why. I guess I simply wasn't thinking straight since the moment Frank woke me.

I stood up.

'I'm going to go to my room and make a call.'

'We'll meet you in Frank's room,' Jack said.

'OK. I'll only be a few minutes.'

THIRTY-SEVEN

I went to my room and called Jerry. He didn't answer. Damn, if I was going to use him as back-up he'd have to catch a plane fast. I'd need to talk to Frank about what was bound to be a heavy airfare on account of the short notice. I was sure he'd cover it.

Since Jack had brought up Jerry I realized I'd automatically agreed to make the drop for Frank without even considering what I was agreeing to. Drops of this kind don't always go smoothly. The kidnappers could kill me and take the money. I needed somebody to back me up and keep me alive, and if it couldn't be Danny, it had to be Jerry. I wouldn't have trusted anyone else.

I decided to go ahead to Frank's room and see what was happening. I'd try Jerry again.

I walked down the hall under the scrutiny of the two FBI men. I wondered how long it was going to take for the kidnappers to call Frank and make their demand. Where was Frankie being held and how was he doing? And I wondered who would be crazy enough to do this, because there was no way Frank would rest until he found them, regardless of whether or not Frankie was returned.

'They're all in there,' one of the men said, as he opened the door for me.

'Thanks.'

As I entered, Frank was saying, '. . . don't feel like it, right now.'

'Frank,' Mickey Rudin said, 'you've got to eat something. You're not gonna do Frankie any good if you pass out from hunger.'

Frank, still seated on the bed by the phone, said, 'Yeah, OK. Have them bring up a table and spaghetti for four. My friends are gonna eat with me.'

'Your friends?' Rudin asked.

'Jack, Eddie and Jilly,' Frank said, 'The rest of you can fend for yourselves.'

The lawyer, who probably considered himself a friend of Frank's, looked a little wounded, but he said, 'OK, I'll take care of it.'

'I'm going to make a few calls,' the DA said. 'I'll check in with you later. If you get a call—'

'Yeah, yeah,' Frank said, 'the FBI's right outside the door. I get it.'

Raggio, Rudin and the FBI left the room. I heard Jack go to the door with them and whisper, 'Make sure there's meatballs.'

When the door closed, Jilly asked Frank, 'You want a drink, Frank?'

'No, I don't want no booze,' Frank said. 'I gotta keep a clear head.'

'Frank, whatever they ask for,' Jack said, 'no matter how much, the Sands will front it.'

'I appreciate that Jack,' Frank said, 'but I got it covered.'

'Frank,' I said, 'I'd like to talk to you about Jerry.'

'Who?'

'Jerry Epstein?'

He frowned at me, almost annoyed, then his face brightened and he said, 'The Brooklyn kid?'

'That's right. I think I'll need him, to back me up on this drop.'

'No problem. Use him.'

'I'll need to get him here – or wherever the drop is supposed to be.'

'Once we get the call and find out, I'll have my plane pick him up. Is he ready?'

'I just have to get him on the phone, but he'll be ready, if I know Jerry,' I said. Knowing he was going to help me *and* Frank, Jerry would walk all the way if he had to . . . barefoot.

'OK, good,' Frank said. 'I want you and Frankie to both walk away from this.'

That made two of us.

I excused myself to try Jerry again, said I'd be back to eat.

This time when I dialed, Jerry answered.

'Hey, what's up, Mr G.?'

I told him about Frank Jr. being kidnapped, and that Frank asked me to make the pay-off.

'I'll be on the first plane to Vegas—'

'No, Jerry,' I said. 'We're in Reno, but I don't want you to come here, either.'

'I gotta do somethin'—'

'And you will,' I said. 'As soon as Frank gets the call with the kidnapper's demands, and finds out where the drop is, he'll send his plane for you. I want you to back me on the drop.'

'You got it, Mr G.' he said. 'Thanks for thinkin' of me.'

'As a matter of fact,' I said, 'I was kind of thinking of me.'

'I getcha. Don't worry, I'll be ready to move as soon as I get the call.'

'Thanks, Jerry,' I said. 'I knew Frank and I could count on you.'

'Always, Mr G. Tell Mr S. I'll see him soon.'

'You got it.'

I hung up, thought about calling Penny in Danny's office and telling her what was going on so she could fill him in. But he was away, working another case, and I didn't want anything leaking out that shouldn't be.

I stepped out into the hall in time to see the two FBI agents frisking the bellman, who stood patiently, probably figuring his tip would make up for it. He had a table on wheels, and there were some folding chairs leaning against the wall that he had probably brought up in the elevator with him.

Finally, they opened the door and allowed the bellman to wheel the table into the room. I came down the hall and grabbed the folding chairs, carrying them in with me.

'That's fine,' Jack Entratter said. 'We'll take care of it.' He tipped the guy a twenty.

'Gee, thanks,' the young man said.

Jilly walked him to the door and ushered him out.

We set the chairs up at the table, and Jack enticed Frank to leave the phone and sit at the table to eat our spaghetti and meatball lunch. Frank backed the table up so he could sit within reach of the phone. He held his fork in his right hand, and the roll of dimes in his left.

When the phone rang we all had our mouths full of pasta. Frank actually spat his out and grabbed the phone.

'Yeah?' he said. 'Yeah, this is him. Is my son . . . what? Wait, is that all? What about—'

Obviously, the person on the other end had hung up. Frank sat there holding the phone, staring.

'Frank,' Jack said. No answer. He got up, walked to Frank and took the phone from him. 'Frank? Who was it? What did they say?'

Frank shook his head, noticed us as if we had just appeared.

'It was them. They said Frankie was OK, and they'd call me again with the amount and the location.'

'That's it?' I asked. 'That's all they said?'

'No,' Frank said, 'he said one more thing.'

'What was it?' Jilly asked.

Frank looked at us and quoted, '"Discretion will be the demeanor."'

THIRTY-EIGHT

The FBI had the phone tapped, but the call hadn't lasted long enough to trace. They did, however, have a tape of the conversation.

Raggio and Rudin came back into the room, leaving the FBI agents in the hall.

'Mr Sinatra,' Raggio said, 'you'll have to keep them on the phone longer next time so we can get a trace.'

'Look, pally,' Frank said, 'I don't care about any damn trace. I want my boy back. I'm gonna pay them, get him back, and then, believe me, I'll find them.'

'Sir,' Raggio said, 'with all due respect—'

Jack Entratter stood up, towering over the DA and the lawyer.

'Mickey, take the gentleman outside so Frank can finish eatin'. When the phone rings again, we'll do our best.'

'Jack—' Rudin said.

'Mickey,' Jack said, 'please.' Jack's tone was respectful, but the look on his face was murderous. Mickey Rudin took the hint and accompanied the DA out into the hall.

'I didn't even get a chance to ask to talk to Frankie,' Frank said.

'It's gonna be OK, Frank,' Jack said. 'They're not gonna hurt Frankie. If they do, they get no money.'

'Jack's right, Frank,' Jilly said. 'They got to keep him healthy, in case you do ask to talk to him, or see him.'

I knew they were trying to make Frank feel better, but none of that rang true to me. They could have killed Frankie already, and still be able to collect from Frank. I was worried because these guys sounded like amateurs. For one thing, they had left a witness alive who could ID them. And they hadn't asked for money yet. It was as if they didn't know how much to ask for and were trying to figure it out.

I wasn't and never have been an expert on kidnapping, but this sounded messy to me.

'All right,' Jack said, 'come on, let's finish eating. You still got to keep your strength up. Next time they call they'll ask for the cash and probably tell you where to deliver it.'

Frank let himself be coaxed into returning to the food, but he mostly played with it from that point on. Actually, it wasn't very good spaghetti. It was way undercooked, and the sauce was watery. The meatballs kept falling apart. Finally we all gave up and pushed the table out into the hall. The FBI men eyed the food hungrily. I never knew if they ate the leftovers or not.

'You guys mind givin' me some time alone?' Frank asked, sometime later.

Why not, I thought? We were just sitting around, doing nothing, anyway. We sure as hell weren't making Frank feel any better.

'Sure, Frank,' Jack said. 'Come on, guys.'

We left the room. The table with the remnants of our meal had been moved. Two FBI men stood there and nodded at us. I wondered what they thought they were guarding.

Jilly and Jack started down the hall to their rooms.

'Hey Jack, I'm gonna go out for some air. I'll be back soon.'

'Yeah, OK, kid,' he said. 'Probably nothin' will happen for a while.'

Even if Frank did get a call about delivering the money there was probably nothing could be done till the next day, anyway.

As I waited for the elevator one of the FBI men said, 'Might not be a good idea to go anywhere.'

'I'll chance it,' I said. 'I just need to stretch my legs.'

'Suit yourself,' he said, with a shrug.

The elevator came and I took it down. In the lobby were the other two FBI men. As I passed, one of them started to speak into a small radio. As I left the hotel I noticed one of them fall into step behind me. Did they really think I was going to contact the kidnappers?

I walked along North Virginia Street past the casinos, beneath the Primadonna's five-lady marquee – not lit up, yet. Foot traffic was brisk, and the FBI man was staying close, since there was no reason for him to try and disguise the fact he was following me.

I kept going until I was passing the Cal-Neva on North Virginia and 2nd Streets. Frank had a piece of the Cal-Neva and had also gotten Dino to invest, but Dean had since sold his interest in the place.

I made a left on 2nd Street and what happened next was probably my own fault. I wasn't paying attention. Maybe I felt secure with an FBI man on my tail, but when a pair of strong hands grabbed me and pulled me into an alley I felt anything but secure.

THIRTY-NINE

They dragged me further into the alley. I struggled but they were two big guys – almost as big as Jerry – and they had a tight hold on me.

Finally, they released me, tossing me against a brick wall. I bounced, but managed to avoid any serious damage – for the time being.

'What the hell!' I said, straightening my jacket. 'What is this, a hold-up?'

'Yeah, a hold-up,' one of them said, pointing to the other one, 'he's gonna hold you up while I beat you senseless.'

'What's the point?' I asked. 'Come on, guys. Is this about the kidnapping?'

The other one played dumb and asked, 'What kidnapping?'

'We don't know what the fuck you're talkin' about,' the first one said. 'This is a message.'

'So spill it.'

'Ya shouldn't oughtta mess with somebody's business,' he told me. 'It ain't healthy.'

'OK fine,' I said, 'message received. I won't mess with anybody's business. Thanks a lot for making me aware . . .'

The two apes exchanged blank looks, then the first one said, 'Huh-uh, that ain't no good, mister. We gotta hurt ya.'

'I don't think you do,' I argued, wondering where the hell the goddamned FBI man was. 'I'm pretty sure I got the message.'

'Naw, we gotta hurt ya some,' the second one said. 'That's what we was told.'

'Otherwise,' the first one said, 'what kinda fun is it?'

'Are you sure you got the right guy?'

'Eddie G., right?' the first one said. 'From the Sands?' Before I could deny that it was me he said, 'Yeah, we got the right guy.'

'Now look,' I said, holding up my hands, 'I know you've got to make a living, but—'

They advanced on me and the first one said, 'Just take it easy.'

The other one grinned and said, 'It's only gonna hurt for about a week.'

There was some daylight between them so I tried to split them and get through, but they grabbed me, threw me against the wall again, only this time harder. The back of my head bounced off the brick and one of them caught me in the gut with a ham-sized fist.

I doubled over, trying to catch my breath, but I knew that wasn't a good posture to be in. I straightened just as one of them launched a haymaker that would have taken my head off if I hadn't dodged it. His fist struck the wall and I heard bones break – lots of 'em, I hoped. He screamed, and they both backed for a minute. That's when I heard somebody yell, 'Hey, hold it!'

The three of us looked up toward the street, the first one cradling his damaged hand.

'FBI!' the guy yelled, and started running towards us,

They took off. The alley cut all the way through to 3rd Street, and they moved pretty quick for big guys.

By the time the FBI guy reached me I had my hands on my knees, bent over, still trying to catch my breath. I was also light headed from having my head slammed against the wall.

'You OK?' he asked, putting his hand on my back.

'I'm . . . I'm . . . I—'

'Yeah, OK,' he said, 'take it easy. Maybe I should go after the—'

I grabbed his arm and shook my head violently, then lost my spaghetti and meatball lunch all over the alley.

FORTY

'So they said nothing about the kidnapping?' the DA asked.

'No,' I said, still rubbing my stomach, 'nothing.'

We were in my room and I was sitting on the bed. Raggio,

Rudin and the FBI agent who had saved me were there, along with Jilly Rizzo and Jack Entratter. Up to that point we had not told Frank what happened.

There was also the hotel doctor in the room, cleaning the gash on the back of my head.

'It won't need stitches,' he said. 'I could shave the area and put a bandage—'

'That's OK, Doc,' I said, waving him away. 'I don't wanna be walking around looking like a monk. Thanks.'

He nodded, closed his bag and left the room.

'So all they said was that they were delivering a message?' Raggio asked.

'Right.'

'And nothing about Frank? Or Frankie?' Rudin asked.

'Not a thing.'

Raggio looked at the FBI agent, whose name was Kent.

'Agent Kent? You didn't hear anything?'

'No,' Kent said. 'I'm sorry, I stopped for a pack of smokes, or I might have been able to save Mr Gianelli some trouble.'

'I think you saved me a lot of pain, Agent Kent. I'm grateful.'

'I'll have to report to the agent in charge,' he said.

'Sure,' Raggio said, 'you go ahead.'

'Mr Gianelli . . . I'm glad you're OK. Again, I'm sorry about the smokes—'

'Never mind,' I said. 'You have my thanks.'

As he left I sipped some water somebody had gotten for me. My throat was sore from losing my lunch. I wished I had a cup of hot coffee.

'Mr Gianelli,' Raggio said, 'is there anything else going on in your life that might explain this? So that we might – and no offense – look past it?'

'I've been thinking about that,' I said. Considering what their message had been – not to mess with anyone's business – I figured the only person whose business I had affected was Barney Irwin. Because of me, his photo studio was closed. 'I think so. I had some—'

Raggio held up his hands and said, 'I don't need to know what it is, especially if it's not in my jurisdiction. I just need to know that this incident has nothing to do with the kidnapping.'

'I'm fairly certain it doesn't.'

'Good.' Raggio and Rudin exchanged a look. 'Then we'll leave you to recover.'

'Yeah, thanks.'

They left the room, leaving me alone with Entratter and Rizzo.

'Jealous husband?' Jilly asked.

'No.'

'Then what?' Jack asked.

'I think this is a holdover of that Abby Dalton thing.'

'Ah . . . I don't know all the facts about that,' Jack said.

'Believe me, you don't need to,' I said. 'I'll take care of this when we get back to Vegas.'

'So you really don't think this is connected to the kidnapping?' Jilly asked.

'No, I don't.'

'OK, then,' Jilly said. 'I'm gonna go back and sit with Frank.'

'We'll be along in a while,' Jack said.

When we were alone, Jack sat on the bed next to me. The mattress sagged significantly.

'You on the level about this?'

'Oh, yeah,' I said. 'They never said a word about the kidnapping, and when I mentioned it they looked confused.'

'You mentioned it?'

'I said the word "kidnapping". That's all. I never mentioned Frank or Frankie.'

'Were they gonna kill you?'

'No,' I said, 'at least, I don't think so. Why lie about a message, and needing to hurt me, if they were plannin' to kill me?'

'And you know who's behind this?'

'I think so,' I said. 'It's a guy who's afraid of Jerry, but apparently not so scared of me.'

'OK,' Jack said, 'OK. I'm glad Agent Kent was on your ass.'

'I wish he'd been a little closer,' I said, rubbing my stomach. 'The worst thing was tasting that spaghetti again.'

'I know,' Jack said. 'That was pretty bad going down. Maybe later we can get a couple of steaks upstairs.'

'I hope their steaks are better than their Italian.'

'The Sky Room is supposed to be pretty good.'

'I hope so.'

'I'm gonna check in with Frank.'

'I'm going to make some calls,' I said. 'I'll see you later.'

He put his hand on my shoulder, squeezed it once, then left. I immediately picked up the phone and dialed Danny's number in Vegas.

FORTY-ONE

'Gorillas?' Danny asked.

'Two of 'em,' I said. 'Big, not smart.'

'Eddie, you just described every hood in the book.'

'From the way they operated I assume they work together all the time,' I said.

'And they look alike?'

'They could wear each other's clothes,' I said. 'In fact . . .'

'What?'

I had just realized, so I said it out loud to see how it sounded.

'. . . they could be brothers.'

'Ah, brothers who work together all the time,' he said. 'That should narrow the field.'

'And they're probably on their way back to Vegas right now.'

'I'll alert both airports,' Danny said. 'Unless they drove, they should be spotted going or coming.'

'Remember,' I said, 'I don't want revenge. I just want to know who they work for.'

'Yeah, but we both figure it's Irwin,' Danny said, 'so what we need to do is follow them.'

'Right,' I said, 'don't brace them . . . alone.'

'What? No, I'm not about to brace two gorillas on my own. Mike Hammer I ain't.'

'OK, good.'

'Now you want to tell me why you're in Reno and what's goin' on?'

'I can tell you,' I said, 'but you can't tell anyone else.'

'You've got my word.'

I told him about Frankie being snatched.

'No demand for cash yet?' he asked.

'No.'

'Sounds like amateur hour,' he said. 'The longer they wait, the more chance there is something can go wrong.'

'I was thinking the same thing!' I said. 'It sounds messy, right?'

'Definitely. Are you sure you want to make the drop?' he asked.

'Why not?' I said. 'They're amateurs, I'm an amateur.'

'Come on, you're practically a card-carrying private eye's assistant.'

'Thanks.'

'You called Jerry, right?'

'I don't call Jerry everytime I get in trou . . . yeah, I called him.'

'Good. The big guy will keep you safe. Stay in touch. Let me know where you are.'

'What are you, my fuckin' father?'

He was laughing when I hung up. I wondered if we had time to get Jerry to Reno before the kidnappers called with their demands? That's when Jack stuck his head in.

'They called.'

FORTY-TWO

When I got to Frank's room the gang was all there. Only the FBI men remained in the hall. Frank was pale and had a stricken look on his face.

'They wouldn't let me talk to him,' he kept saying. 'They wouldn't . . .'

Raggio looked at me and said, 'They insisted that Frank Jr. is fine.'

'Did they say how much they want?'

'Yes,' Raggio said, 'and we don't understand it.'

'Why?'

'They asked for two hundred and forty thousand dollars.'

'What? That's all?'

'They could have asked for millions,' Jilly Rizzo said. 'Frank would have paid it.'

'That's hard to understand,' Jack Entratter said.

'What about the location?' I asked.

'All they said was,' Raggio said, 'they wanted Mr Sinatra to go to LA.'

'OK,' I said, 'at least we know that much.'

'He's going to fly back tomorrow,' Entratter said to me. 'You can go with him.'

'Fine. I'll call Jerry. He can fly to LA and meet us at the airport.'

'Work it out with him,' Jack said. 'I'll make sure the two pilots are coordinated.'

'OK.'

'Go,' Jack said, 'make the call, and then come back. Frank'll be able to talk then.'

I backed out of the room, went to mine and made the call.

I made the arrangements with Jerry to fly to LA in the morning.

'You can join us at the airport,' I said. 'I'm not sure where we'll go from there. Frank will have to decide where he wants to stay.'

'I'll be there, Mr G.'

'And since you'll be flying on Frank's private plane,' I said, 'bring your gun, Jerry.'

'I hear ya.'

'Let me fill you in on something else.' I went on to tell him about the two hoods who had attacked me on the street.

'They musta followed you there, Mr G., intendin' to deliver that message.'

'Pretty nervy,' I said, 'or pretty dumb, with the FBI around.'

'Well,' he said, 'you did put yourself out there, didn't ya?'

'I did, yeah,' I admitted. 'Luckily, one of the feds followed me, or who knows what would've happened. They might have beaten me to death.'

'I don't think they woulda killed you, Mr G.,' Jerry said, disagreeing with me. 'They probably woulda just messed ya up some.'

'Unless they're the same ones who killed Wayne in Vegas.'

'Well, I agree with you that it probably had nothin' to do with the kidnappin'. Maybe we'll have to go back to Vegas and find that Irwin guy. I'll have to make an even bigger impression on him.'

'First things first, Jerry,' I said. 'We've got to get Frankie back.'

'Yes, sir, we do,' Jerry said. 'I'll see you tomorrow mornin', Mr G. You tell Mr S. to hang on, 'cause I'm comin'.'

'See ya, big guy. Watch your back.'

'I always do.'

I hung up, called Danny's number next. He wasn't there but I told Penny I'd be in LA the next day, and would call from there to give them a number where they could reach me.

'Watch yourself, Eddie G.,' she said, before we hung up.

'I'll do my best, doll.'

After I hung up I sat there for a few moments. I needed some time to myself. My head was pounding, my gut still ached, and it was starting to hit me that Frank Jr.'s life might be at least partially in my hands. That made me nervous as hell. But I was bolstered by the fact that, of all the people Frank could have chosen to do this, he chose me. Nothing I'd ever done for him before had ever been as personal as this, and I was determined to come through for him.

I stood up, shook my arms out, stretched and then figured – with the help of some aspirin – I could get right back into the game.

FORTY-THREE

It came down to me, Jack Entratter, Jilly Rizzo and Frank in his room, first drinking coffee, and then ordering some bourbon from room service. I took the opportunity to tell Frank about Jerry meeting us in the morning.

'That's good,' he said. 'I want him to make sure the exchange goes down perfect, and you get back safe.'

'Where will you be staying in LA, Frank?' Jack asked.

'I called Nancy,' Frank said. 'I'm gonna stay in her house in Bel-Air. When we get Frankie back I'll have him brought there. His mother and sisters are worried.'

'Everybody's worried, Frank,' Jilly said.

'I know,' Frank said. 'The word's got out.'

'How'd that happen?' Jack asked.

'You know, Jack,' Frank said. 'This kind of thing is hard to keep a lid on. I got some calls offering to help.'

'From who?' Jilly asked.

'Bobby Kennedy, for one.'

'What?' Entratter said, shocked. 'What did the boy Attorney General want?'

'He said if there was anything him or his family could do, I should let them know.'

'Have you heard from them since Jack was killed?' Jilly asked. 'Since they wouldn't let you go to the funeral?'

'No,' Frank said, 'this was the first time.'

'What did you tell him?' I asked.

'I said I appreciated his offer, but that me and my people had the situation in hand.'

'You know who he's gonna think you mean by your people, don't you?' Jilly asked.

'I don't give a rat's ass what he thinks,' Frank said. 'As a matter of fact, I also got a call from Mo Mo.'

'What'd he say?' Jack asked.

'Pretty much the same thing. If I need any help, give him a call.'

If Frank had allowed Giancana to get involved, the kidnappers probably would end up dead.

'And what'd you tell him?' Jilly asked.

Frank actually smiled, but just for a second.

'Pretty much the same thing. I don't need either one of them gettin' involved. I just want to pay the ransom and get my boy back.'

'We all want that, Frank,' Jilly said.

'We better turn in,' Jack said. 'We have to get an early start in the mornin'.'

'Are we all going?' I asked.

'Yeah,' Jack said. 'Jilly and me, we're stickin' until the kid is back home safe and sound.'

'I appreciate that,' Frank said, 'but Jack's right. And I need to talk to Eddie for a little bit, alone. So you two get out.'

Frank was kicking Jilly and Jack out as nicely as he could. The bottle was empty, so they didn't put up much of a fight.

When the door closed behind them Frank said, 'Any coffee left in that pot?'

I picked it up and shook it.

'A little.'

'Pour it out, kid,' Frank said.

I poured and handed him his cup.

'What's up, Frank?'

'Just wanna give you a chance to back out, Eddie,' he said. 'You might be puttin' your life on the fuckin' line, here. Jerry's flyin' in, he can do the swap if you'd rather not.'

'Frank, I said I was in, and I am. I'm not going to change my mind.'

'You're a good friend, Eddie,' he said. 'A good friend. If we get Frankie back – what am I saying? When we get Frankie back you got a big fuckin' thank you comin' to you.'

'It'll be enough for me to see that kid safe and sound.'

'Yeah, well, we'll see,' Frank said. 'You just might find somethin' nice on your doorstep. Somethin' real nice.'

'Frank, I don't—'

Frank drained his cup and slapped me on the shoulder.

'Now get out of here so I can get some sleep. We'll meet in the lobby at seven a.m.'

'Seven,' I said. 'I'll be there.' I put my cup down, untouched. It was cold, anyway.

I left the room, walked past two of the FBI men and entered my room.

'Eddie.'

I jumped. I hadn't expected to see anybody in my room, so the DA, Bill Raggio, scared the shit out of me.

'Close the door, Eddie,' Raggio said, standing up from the bed, where he'd been seated. 'We have to talk.'

FORTY-FOUR

I closed the door, locked it, and turned to face the DA.

'What's this about, Mr Raggio?'

'You know what it's about, Eddie,' he said. 'The exchange. We want it to go off without a hitch.'

'Without a hitch is what I want, too,' I said. 'Who's we?'

'Me and the FBI.'

'And why wouldn't it go off without a hitch?' I asked. 'I'm going to do exactly what Frank wants me to do.'

'That's what we're afraid of,' Raggio said.

I stared at him, but he didn't offer anything more than that.

'I'm afraid I don't understand, Mr Raggio,' I said. 'What are you getting at?'

He started to pace, as if forming his thoughts.

'The kidnappers,' he said, finally, 'we want them alive.'

'What are you—' I started, then realized what he was saying. 'Wait a minute. You think . . . I'm not a killer, Mr Raggio. Where did you get that idea?'

'You work at the Sands, don't you?' he asked. 'For Entratter?'

'Sure I do,' I said, 'as a pit boss.'

'Come on, Eddie. I checked you out today. I spoke to Detective Hargrove with the Vegas PD. He filled me in on your history.'

'My history?'

'When you and some Brooklyn thug named Jerry are around, bodies pile up.' Raggio pointed his finger at me. 'Why else would Frank Sinatra send for you to get his kid back? Well, I'm telling you now, I want those kidnappers, and I want them alive.'

'Mr Raggio—'

'I can't go to LA with you tomorrow. That's out of my jurisdiction. But I'm going to call ahead to the DA there. The cops are going to be watching you.'

'That's fine with me, Mr Raggio,' I said. 'You tell 'em to do their job, and I'll do mine.'

'And what is your job, Eddie?'

'Right now it's to help Frank get his son back. And I don't intend to kill anybody while I do it.'

'So you say,' Raggio said. 'Now you take this as a warning—'

'And take this as a warning,' I said, too pissed to worry about consequences. 'Get out of here before I throw you out.'

'Just remember what I said, Gianelli.'

'You remember what I said, Raggio,' I retorted. 'Get out.'

Without another word Raggio left. Moments later there was a knock on the door. I considered not answering it, just in case it was him again. Or maybe this time it was the FBI wanting to 'warn' me.

In the end, I opened it. It was Jack Entratter.

'Can I come in?'

'Sure.'

He entered, closed the door behind him.

'I saw Raggio leavin',' he said. 'He didn't look happy.'

'He was here to warn me.'

'About what?'

'He says he wants the kidnappers alive,' I said. 'Seems he thinks Frank is sendin' me to kill 'em.'

'What?'

'I know. I told him to get out. But he's gonna cause trouble, Jack. He said he's going to call ahead to the LA District Attorney.'

'Where did he get that idea?'

'From Hargrove.'

'That bastard! What's he got to do with this?'

'Raggio checked me out with him. He seems to think since I work for you and the Sands – and I'm friends with Frank – that I'm mobbed up.'

'Then I guess it's a good thing Frank didn't accept Mo Mo's offer of help,' Entratter said. 'That would've sealed it for him.'

'And maybe he should have accepted Bobby's offer,' I said. 'That would have kept the cops at bay.'

'Frank's made his decision,' Jack said. 'All we can do is go along.'

I hesitated a moment, then said, 'I agree.'

'What about the other thing?' he asked. 'The two mugs who grabbed you?'

'I've got Danny Bardini working on it,' I said. 'When I get back to Vegas we'll take care of it.'

'OK,' Jack said, slapping me on the back. 'Get some sleep. I'll make some calls of my own to LA. Since Raggio checked you out, it might make sense for us to check him out.'

FORTY-FIVE

Frank's plane was a Martin 404. It had been introduced in 1962, had a cruising speed of 280 mph, and a high speed of 312 mph. I knew all that because Frank told us the night before.

The 404 was a small business plane that Frank used often, and loaned out to his friends. I knew that Dean used it to fly to concerts and business meetings. He had also loaned it on occasion to every other member of the group.

We met in the lobby at seven a.m. and took two cars to the airport. The plane was gassed up and ready to go, props already turning. Raggio stayed behind. The lawyer, Rudin, was with us, and two FBI agents – my hero one of them. So that made seven of us.

We followed Frank up the airstair and inside. We hadn't stopped for breakfast, or even coffee, but Frank had us served coffee and bagels on board. I wondered if Jerry was getting the same treatment on the plane Frank had sent for him. The pilot had been told to operate at high speed. We'd be in LA within the hour.

The flight was pretty quiet. I didn't have a chance to talk with Jack about the night before. I didn't know yet if either one of us was even going to mention it to Frank. Certainly not in front of the FBI agents.

Rudin led us off the plane at the other end. The District Attorney was waiting for us, along with some local cops and two more FBI agents. He and Rudin shook hands, seemed to know each other, Rudin then introduced him to Frank. The rest of us didn't rate.

There were two cars waiting for us, and Jerry was standing beside one of them. I walked over to join him while Rudin and the DA talked.

'Hey, Mr G.'

'Hey, Jerry. Been here long?'

'About fifteen minutes,' the big guy said. 'I'm starvin'.'

'Have anything on the plane?'

'Some coffee and donuts,' Jerry said. ''Bout a dozen.'

'You ate them all?'

'I had a longer flight than you.'

'Good point.'

'I'm still hungry, though.'

'We'll get something.'

'Where are we goin'?'

'Mrs Sinatra's house in Bel-Air.'

'The ex?'

'That's right.'

'Guess she must be worried.'

'Out of her mind.'

Entratter and Jilly walked over to us and said, 'We're in this car.'

'OK,' I said. 'You guys know Jerry, right?'

'Yeah,' Entratter said. 'Hello, Jerry.'

'Mr Entratter,' Jerry said. 'Hello, Mr Rizzo.'

'Hey, Jerry. How you doin'?'

'Good. Hungry.'

'Tell me about it.'

'We'll eat when we get to Nancy's house,' Entratter said. He looked at the driver. 'Let's go.'

'Yessir.'

We piled into the car, which, thankfully, had enough room for the three of us and Jerry. Oddly, Jerry was able to somehow make himself smaller and take up only a corner. I never knew how he did it, but the big boy rarely seemed to intrude. His size never became an issue when he was with friends.

'Eddie, I told Jilly what happened last night between you and Raggio.'

'OK.'

'What happened?' Jerry asked.

I told him.

'Jilly and I feel it's better if we don't tell Frank,' Jack said, after I was finished.

'Makes sense,' I said. 'Why give him something else to worry about?'

'Right,' Jilly said.

'And I made some calls,' Jack said to me. 'I think I made sure the local DA will stay off your back.'

'That would be good.'

'Rudin and the DA – Evans is his name – are tight. They play poker together. So we kept him out of it.'

'Again,' I said, 'makes sense.'

'OK,' Jack said, looking at me, Jerry and then Jilly, 'so we don't mention this at all while we're in Nancy's house.'

We all agreed.

'What are we gonna eat when we get there?' Jerry asked.

Jilly laughed and said, 'Don't worry, Jerry. Whatever it is, you'll get enough.'

FORTY-SIX

When we got to Nancy's house she greeted us politely. Frank hugged her and took her off to talk in private.

'There's food in the kitchen,' she told us.

'Thank you, Nancy,' Entratter said.

We went to the kitchen, followed by the two FBI men, but they stopped at the door. The table was covered, buffet style, with plates filled with eggs, bacon, potatoes and – to Jerry's delight – pancakes.

Entratter, Jilly Rizzo, Jerry and I filled our plates, and then Jack turned to the FBI men and said, 'Have at it, boys.'

The two men exchanged glances. One of them said, 'Thank you, sir.'

We stood around eating and after a while the lawyer, Rudin, arrived with the DA and some technicians who were going to wire Nancy's phone.

'Is that smart?' Entratter asked.

'The kidnappers will expect it,' Rudin said, 'unless they're hopeless amateurs.'

That seemed likely to me, but I didn't say anything.

The DA and his techs went into the living room to wire the phones. Rudin grabbed a plate and had some breakfast.

'Where are the girls?' I asked Entratter.

'Nancy and Tina are upstairs,' Jack said. 'They're stayin' out of the way.'

'Anybody with them?' I asked. 'I mean, in case somebody tries to grab them, too?'

'Frank's got Ed Pucci and some other bodyguards on 'em,' Jack said.

I had heard Pucci's name before, but never met him.

'I'm glad he's got them covered.'

'He's not about to let one of his girls get grabbed,' Jilly said. 'Not after what happened with Frankie.'

The conversation stopped when Frank came into the kitchen.

'You guys get enough to eat?' he asked.

'There's plenty, Mr S.,' Jerry said, piling his plate high with more pancakes. I stood next to him and took some food.

'Mr G.?' Jerry said, lowering his voice.

'Yeah, Jerry?'

'Can we find a corner alone?' he asked. 'I gotta tell you somethin'.'

I looked at him with a joke on my lips, but I saw that he was serious.

'It's a big house,' I said. 'Got to be lots of corners.'

We both added bacon to our plates, and left the kitchen. We found two chairs at the end of a hall and sat down.

'What's up?'

'You know those two mugs who grabbed you in Reno?'

'Yeah.'

'Same thing happened to me in Brooklyn, after we talked.'

'What?'

'Yup,' he said, 'only there was three of 'em.'

'Jesus,' I said. 'What happened? Did you get hurt?'

'Well,' Jerry said, 'I'll tell you . . .'

Jerry said they came for him right in his house. He got back from doing some grocery shopping, entered his house with two bags. They jumped him as soon as he got in the door.

Something hit him from behind and he went sprawling, cans of vegetables and packages of meat flying everywhere.

Jerry, being a pro, immediately rolled, avoiding the size-fourteen boot that tried to stomp him.

He kept rolling and came to his feet at the other end of the room, holding the nearest thing he could grab. There were three of them facing him, and they had knives. All he had in his hand was a frozen whole chicken.

Whether they were there to kill him or mess him up he didn't know, but he treated it like he'd treat any attack – like it was deadly. So he wasn't going to hold back.

But they were pros. Jerry had seen lots of TV and movie fights where the hero was outnumbered, but the bad guys rushed him one at a time. In real life it didn't work that way. Bad guys tended to use their superior numbers to their advantage.

The three of them – all as big as rhinos – charged him.

Jerry did the unexpected.

He charged them, too, his arms outstretched. At the last moment he left his feet in a leap, crashed into the three of them, taking all four of them to the floor. This time he was ready. As he landed he swung his chicken, hitting one of them in the head. Jerry had swung with all his might, so when frozen chicken met guy's head, the head cracked like a coconut.

That left two.

Jerry rolled away and came to his feet, again. He hadn't had a chance to grab the downed hood's knife, so he was still armed with his chicken.

The other two scrambled to get to their feet. As they did one of them stepped on their fallen comrade's foot. He staggered, and Jerry leaped at the chance to take advantage. Long ago Jerry had learned to use his size and weight to his advantage. He bulled into the other man with his shoulder, sending him staggering back, then swung his deadly chicken again.

That left one.

This time he bent over and picked up the man's knife . . .

'And?' I asked.

'I took care of the third guy,' he said.

'All three? Dead?'

'All three.'

'How'd you avoid the cops?'

'I called a cleaner.'

A 'cleaner' was somebody who did just what the name implied – cleaned up a mess like that without cops getting involved.

'So Irwin is so scared he sent goons to kill both of us,' I said.

'Guess maybe I didn't scare him enough last time,' Jerry said.

'Or too much. When we get back to Vegas we're gonna find his ass and ask him.'

At that point Frank came down the hall toward us.

'Let's keep this between us for now,' I said.

'OK.'

'Eddie? Can I talk to you?' Frank asked.

'Sure.' My plate was almost empty, anyway, so I set it down and followed Frank into the dining room, where he stopped and faced me.

'I want you to meet the LA county DA,' he said. 'We'll be working closely with him.'

'Fine.'

'I mentioned your name to him, and he flinched,' Frank said. 'Plus, I know when there's somethin' that's not bein' told to me, get it?'

'I get it, Frank.'

'So what the hell's goin' on?'

I told him about Raggio talking with Detective Hargrove, and then calling Evans.

'I get it,' he said, 'I get it. That Raggio, he's an ignorant SOB.'

'Obviously.'

'OK,' he said, 'let's go and talk to the DA, see what he's got to say.'

'OK.'

Frank put his arm around me.

'We all gotta work together to get Frankie home,' he said, 'and it ain't gonna work if we don't trust each other.'

'Yeah, well,' I said, 'tell that to the DA.'

'I am,' he said. 'Right now. Let's go.'

FORTY-SEVEN

'Eddie,' Frank said, when we got to the living room, 'this is District Attorney Douglas Evans.'

Evans was a smooth-faced man in his forties, with a perfect haircut and an expensive suit. He put his hand out and after a moment I shook it.

'This is Eddie Gianelli, Doug,' Frank said. 'He's gonna make the delivery for me.'

'Pleased to meet you, Eddie,' Evans said.

'I think you've heard of Eddie before, haven't you, Doug?' Frank asked.

Evans blinked. 'I'm sorry?'

'I said you've heard Eddie's name before,' Frank said.

Evans looked over at the lawyer, Rudin, who just shrugged.

'Yeah,' Frank said, 'Raggio, from Nevada, he called you about Eddie. Told you some things that I think may not be true.'

'I usually make my own decisions and opinions, Mr Sinatra,' Evans said, smoothly. 'If my Nevada counterpart did call me, I'm sure he was just trying to be helpful.'

'I just want you to know I trust this man completely,' Frank said, pointing at me. 'I trust him to do the right thing.'

'That's good enough for me, Mr Sinatra,' Evans said. 'My priority is to get your son back safely. I'm sure Mr Gianelli intends to do everything he can to make sure that happens.'

'I do,' I said. I couldn't think of anything else to say. I didn't find Evans to be as distasteful or stupid as the Nevada DA, Raggio, but I was leaving room for error on my part.

'Mr Sinatra—' Evans said.

'Just call me Frank, Doug,' Frank said. 'It'll make things easier.'

'Frank, we'll need you to stay here by the phone—'

'Don't worry,' Frank said, 'I'm not going anywhere.'

But he was.

A call came in an hour later, and the voice – according to Frank the same voice as the other calls – told him to go to a pay phone somewhere in LA and make a call.

We were all sitting around at that point, so we heard Frank's end of the conversation.

'I'll send a man with you, Frank—' Evans said, but Frank cut him off.

'No,' he said, 'I'll take Eddie.'

'He's not a cop,' Evans said, 'and I assume he's not armed—'

'And I don't have the money on me,' Frank said. 'They're not gonna try anythin' funny. They just want to run me around a little. I'm willing to do anything for Frankie.'

Evans didn't like it, but Frank was adamant.

'What about me, Mr S.?' Jerry asked.

'I appreciate the offer, Jerry, but I'll just take Eddie.' He looked at me. 'You ready?'

Obviously, somebody had brought Frank's black-on-black Ghia L6.4.

'You drive,' he said, tossing me the key. The Ghia was a powerful sports car, and the engine growled when I turned the key. Under other circumstances I would have enjoyed driving that car.

'In case anybody's watching,' he said to me as we started out, 'I'll say you're my driver.'

'OK, Frank.'

He had the roll of dimes in his left hand, flexing and unflexing around it. He had to direct me, since I didn't know my way around.

They had told Frank to go to a pay phone on North Beverly Glen Boulevard. When we got there it was obvious why. It was sitting out in the open along the side of the road, surrounded by hills. Anyone could keep watch from a distance without being seen.

'Stay in the car,' he told me.

I watched him take a dime from his pocket and drop it in the phone. It did not come from the roll of dimes. He still held that in his left hand.

He dialed, waited, spoke briefly, then hung up. When he came back he was scowling.

'They're playin' games,' he said. 'Drive.'

I drove.

'They sound like amateurs, Frank.'

'That's what I'm afraid of,' he said. 'With pros I'd be fairly confident about gettin' Frankie back safe. But now, with these guys . . . Eddie, I just don't know.'

'Look, Frank,' I said, 'let's do what they tell us to do. Whatever, to get Frankie back. That's all we've got.'

'Yeah, OK,' Frank said. 'Drive.'

He directed me to the next phone booth.

They ran us around to three more phone booths. Eventually, Frank had to crack his roll of dimes. Finally, they told us to go back to the house. I guess they had satisfied themselves that we didn't have cops following us wherever we went.

As we drove to Bel-Air I asked, 'How did they have the phone number of the house in Bel-Air in the first place?'

'I gave it to them,' Frank said, 'the last call in Reno.'

'So they're gonna call you there again?'

Frank nodded.

'That's when they'll tell me where to bring the money,' he said.

'And that's what we'll do,' I said. 'But we'll need a bigger car.'

Frank frowned at me.

'No way is Jerry gonna fit in the trunk of this one.'

Frank actually laughed.

FORTY-EIGHT

When we got back to the house I let Frank brief the others on what we'd been doing. Somebody handed me a bottle of beer, which I appreciated.

'Was anybody watching you?' Evans asked.

Frank looked at me.

'I didn't see anybody, but I'd say yeah. I mean, otherwise what was the point of running us from phone to phone?'

'Good point,' Evans said.

I looked around the room. There were more people there than when we left. More cops. More FBI. I found out later there were better than a hundred cops and two dozen FBI agents out looking for Frankie.

'OK,' Evans said, 'so we're back to waiting for a call.'

'I don't want it traced,' Frank said.

'What?'

'Stop trying to trace the calls,' Frank said. 'I just want to pay the money and get my kid.'

'Mr Sinatra,' Evans said, 'we're very experienced at this—'

'That's why I think I'll go with payin',' Frank said.

'I don't understand.'

'Really?' Frank asked. 'Jerry understands, don't you, Jerry?'

Jerry had been standing to the side. Now he stepped up, and suddenly he seemed to fill the room.

'You're all pros,' he said, 'used to dealin' with pros. These guys are amateurs. They ain't doin' what you expect 'em to do.'

'That's right,' Frank said.

'Makes sense,' Rudin said.

'Send your men home, Mr Evans,' Frank said. 'You can stay if you want, keep as many men here as you want. Send the wire men home. I'm gonna pay.'

'Mr Sinatra—'

'It's my kid,' Frank said, 'and my call.'

The room got quiet. We all turned our eyes to the doorway, where Nancy was standing. She'd heard everything Frank said.

'Excuse me.' Frank walked to Nancy and they went into another room.

'All right, boys,' DA Evans said, 'let's pack it all up.'

Jerry looked at me. I jerked my head for him to follow me and we went to the kitchen. A new spread had been put out for lunch.

'That's real turkey,' Jerry said. He started building himself a sandwich. After all the running around with Frank, I was ready for one, too.

'I don't know how this happened, Jerry,' I said, 'but this is gonna fall to you and me.'

'I know, Mr G.'

'Are you ready?' I asked.

'I'm always ready, Mr G.,' he said, 'you know that.' He added cheese to his sandwich, lettuce, mayo, pickles, built it higher than my mouth would have been able to handle. Mine was half the size.

He took a bite.

'I know you are, Jerry,' I said.

'So are you, Mr G.,' Jerry said. 'I know that, so does Mr S. You gotta believe it, is all.'

He was right. I took a bite of my sandwich.

FORTY-NINE

If we had been at Frank's house we probably would have all just sacked out on the floor, or a sofa, or some kind of chair. But we were at Nancy's place, so Frank gave Jerry and me a car and told us where the nearest motel was.

'You'll be able to get here in five minutes,' he assured us.

He actually gave us one of the limos, which Jerry drove to the Bel-Air Motor Court. We decided just to go ahead and get one room with two double beds, so that when the call came in we'd both know it.

There were vending machines in the lobby and when we got to the room Jerry dumped his load of chips, pretzels and candy on one of the beds, thereby claiming it as his. We also had a Styrofoam cup of coffee each which we got from a nearby coffee shop.

There was a TV in the room, and while we did turn it on we left the volume low. Jerry offered me my choice of potato chips, corn chips or pretzels to go with my coffee, and I chose pretzels. He didn't look happy about it, but if he didn't want to lose them he shouldn't have offered.

We each sat on our respective beds to wait for the phone to ring.

'What's happening with Billy?' I asked.

'I don't know what to do about that kid, Mr G.,' he said. 'Spends most of his time workin' on that system. I got him to pay back part of that dough he owes the Sands, but he keeps sayin' he's waitin' to hit big so he can pay it all back.'

'He's got time.'

'I appreciate you talkin' to Mr Entratter about that, Mr G.'

'Don't worry,' I said. 'Jack's got other things on his mind. Just don't bring Billy back to Vegas for a while.'

'Don't worry,' Jerry said. 'When he swiped that dough I crossed him off my list.'

'What list?'

'The list of people I'd bring to Vegas with me.'

'So how long is the list now?'

He thought a moment, then said, 'Nobody. He was the only one. And that was only because my aunt asked me to do it.'

'Did you tell your aunt what he did?' I asked. 'Lost seventy grand, tried to get more credit from another casino, stole five Gs from you and tried to gamble it? All that?'

'I did,' Jerry said. 'I ratted him out, sang like a canary.'

'I'll bet he didn't like that.'

'I don't know if he even cares,' Jerry said. 'I don't know if you noticed, but he ain't exactly the sharpest knife in the drawer, ya know?'

'I know.'

'Wait a minute, wait a minute,' Jerry said. He sprang off the bed and turned the volume up on the TV. 'I love this movie.' He returned to the bed.

I looked at the screen and saw the title JOHNNY CONCHO. It was Frank's first film as a director, where he also played the title character.

'Yeah, I like this, too.'

'Let's watch it!' Jerry sprang off the bed again. 'I'll go get some Cokes.'

As he ran out the door I called out, 'See if you can find some popcorn.'

FIFTY

The phone rang early the next morning. Jerry moaned and I rolled over and grabbed it.

'Get over here,' Frank said, and hung up.

I hopped out of bed and slapped Jerry on the shoulder.

'Gotta go, big guy.'

He groaned, but got his feet around to the floor while I was pulling on my pants. He reached under his pillow and brought out his .45. For once I was glad to see it.

He drove the limo to Nancy's house in Bel-Air. There was a wall of reporters and cameras outside.

'Looks like the word is out,' I said.

'Hold on.'

He expertly worked his way through the crowd without hitting anyone . . . too hard. A couple of men – probably Sinatra's bodyguards – opened the gates to let us through.

Inside the house there was a lot of activity, none of it seeming to accomplish anything. Frank was talking to a man who appeared to have arrived just before us.

'Eddie,' he said, when he spotted me, 'this is Al Hart, from my bank. He brought the money.'

'Where is it?'

Frank picked up a brown paper bag and showed it to me.

'This is the way they want it,' he said.

'Fine. When do we go?'

'Now,' Frank said.

'There are a hell of a lot of reporters outside, Frank.'

'I know,' he said. 'You drive. I'll crouch down in the back.'

'I'll get in the trunk,' Jerry said.

Evans, who was standing by listening, asked, 'Do you think you'll fit?'

Jerry tossed him a look and said, 'I'll make myself fit.'

'Where are we supposed to go?' I asked.

'I'll tell you when we get in the car.'

'Mr Sinatra,' Evans said, 'if you'll tell me I can have some men—'

'No,' Frank said, 'no men. If these guys are amateurs, seeing a bunch of cops might make them kill Frankie.'

'Sir, with all due respect, they might kill him anyway.'

'I'm bettin' two hundred and forty thou they won't – and this ain't the biggest bet I ever made. Just the most important.' He turned and thrust the paper bag of loot into my hands. 'Let's go.'

Frank, Jerry and I marched out to the car. I used the key to open the trunk for Jerry.

'You got your piece, Jerry?' Frank asked.

'Yes, sir.'

'Good,' Frank said, 'so do I.' He was wearing a wrinkled grey suit, as if he'd slept in it, a white shirt, no tie. He opened the jacket and showed us the revolver in his belt. Jerry and I were similarly clad in wrinkled jackets. We all needed a shave. All we needed was some booze on us to complete the look of winos.

'Frank,' I said, 'is that a good idea?'

'If they hurt Frankie, Eddie,' he said. 'Or . . . or worse, I'll kill 'em.' He gave me a hard look. 'And don't get in my way.'

'I won't, Frank.'

His look softened, then he touched my arm and said, 'You're a good friend – both of you are.'

'Anything for you, Mr S.,' Jerry said.

'Good, big guy. Now get in the trunk.'

After we got away from the house and the reporters, Frank told me where we were going.

'Phone booths,' he said. 'If I'm any good at guessing, there'll be a coupla stops.'

'Again?'

'I'm sure once they're satisfied that we're not being watched they'll tell me where to deliver the money.'

'OK.'

'But pull over here, first,' he said. We were on a stretch of deserted highway. 'We'll let Jerry out before he suffocates. He can crouch down in back and I'll sit up front with you.'

'Gotcha.'

I pulled over and let Frank out. He released Jerry from the trunk. They both got situated and I started driving again.

'This is it, guys,' Frank said. 'This is where we either get Frankie back, or I'm gonna end up killin' somebody.'

I hoped with all my heart that the first part was true, and the last part would never happen.

FIFTY-ONE

The kidnappers ran us around LA until finally, at the last phone booth, Frank got excitedly back into the car.

'OK, we got it,' he said. 'Sunset Boulevard.'

'What?'

'That's what they said. "Leave the money between two school buses parked at a gas station on Sunset Boulevard."'

'Where on Sunset?'

'Just drive,' Frank said, 'I'll tell you where.'

He directed me, and we finally arrived at the site. I parked across the street. We sat there for a few moments.

'OK,' he said. 'Gimme the money.'

The bag was on the back seat with Jerry. He picked it up and passed it to Frank.

'Frank,' I said, 'do you want me to—'

'No,' he said. 'If they're watchin' I want them to see me deliver it. Just sit tight, boys.'

He got out of the car, crossed the street, walking quickly. I had the feeling it was all he could do not to break into a run. Frank Jr. might have been just feet away from him.

Frank looked around, set the package down, and hurried back to the car.

'I couldn't see anything,' he said, getting in.

'Neither did we,' I said.

'What now?' Jerry asked.

'Back to the house.'

'Mr S.,' Jerry said, 'Mr G. can pull around the block, and I can come back on foot to watch—'

'No, Jerry,' Frank said. 'We'll go home to wait for a call, or for Frankie to come home.'

'Whatever you say, Frank.'

I started the car and headed to Bel-Air.

Once again we worked our way through the reporters to get to the house. Afterward, we just sat around and waited, as Frank asked us to. It was quite a motley crowd. Those of us who were part of Frank's circle all looked alike: unshaven and rumpled. The policeman and FBI agents were clean and sharply dressed. We all wore the same hangdog expression.

A few hours later a policeman came into the room to whisper into DA Evans' ear. Evans then came over to Frank and, within earshot of me, said, 'We should go to the front door.'

'What for?'

'Come on, Frank.'

Evans and Frank started, I followed, Jerry followed me, and then suddenly everyone – Entratter, Jilly Rizzo, the FBI men, cops, bodyguards, Rudin – trudged to the front door.

Since I was right behind Frank I had a clear view of the driveway. A patrol car drove up and stopped in front of the house.

'What's goin' on?' Frank asked.

A lone patrolman got out of the car, walked to the back and opened the trunk. As if by magic, Frank Jr. stepped out.

'Oh my God!' Frank said, and ran to him. As we all watched he gave the boy a bone-crushing hug, which had Frankie grinning shyly. Or maybe he was just embarrassed by the attention. I figured he was gonna have to face a lot more from his mother and sisters.

Frank dragged the boy into the house as we all added back slaps and applause.

The prodigal son was home.

FIFTY-TWO

After about seventy-four hours of panic, the mood in the house lifted sky high.

Bobby Kennedy called to tell Frank how glad he was Frank Jr. was home. Frank was very polite and thanked him for his concern, and again for his offer of help.

Frank called his mother, Dolly, to tell her that her grandson was home and safe.

Frank Jr. had to sit with the DA and the FBI, who subjected him to some rigorous questioning, in an attempt to get enough facts to catch the kidnappers. I was listening to the interview, as most of us were, when Frankie mentioned that he was held in a house in Canoga Park. He also said the kidnappers referred to each other by their first names: Joe, Barry, and Johnny.

It hit me then like a clap of thunder.

I pulled Jerry aside.

'What?' he asked.

'That piece of paper I found in Barney Irwin's desk had those names on it.'

'What names?'

'Barry. Johnny. And Canoga Park.'

'Do you have it on you?'

'No, damn it,' I said, 'it's at my place.'

'Whataya think it means?'

'I don't know,' I said. 'There was some other stuff on it, too, but I can't remember.'

'You wanna tell the FBI? And the DA?'

'If I tell them, it'll get back to that ass, Raggio,' I said. 'I don't wanna help him, at all.'

'So what do we do?' Jerry wanted to know.

I rubbed my jaw, gave it some thought.

'Frankie's home,' I said. 'There's nothin' we can do here about findin' the kidnappers. So we head back to Vegas, check out that note, and find Barney Irwin. Figure out what his involvement is, if any. And maybe we can also find out who killed Wayne. If I can I'd like to hand that killer to Hargrove on a platter. And, hopefully, Irwin's right in the middle of it all. Including the attacks on us.'

'OK, so when do we leave?'

'Now,' I said. 'I'll talk to Frank about his plane.'

'OK,' Jerry said, 'I'm with you, Mr G.'

'Thanks, Jerry.'

I went to find Frank.

Frank agreed to have his plane take us back to Vegas. He was so happy about having Frankie home, he didn't even ask why.

'You did a great job, pally,' he said, hugging me, 'A great job. I owe you, big time.'

I stopped by Entratter's side and told him what we were doing.

'Good idea,' he said. 'I'll come with you.'

'We're leavin' now,' I said.

'What's the hurry?'

'I'll tell you when we're on the plane.'

'OK, lemme say goodbye to Frank.'

Frank gave us a limo and a driver to run us out to the airport. In an hour and a half we were back at the Sands.

During the plane ride I had given Entratter all the facts. Or so I thought.

'But you don't have any facts, Eddie,' Jack said. 'Where's that piece of paper?'

'At home,' I said, 'somewhere.'

'It better have more on it than you remember,' he said. 'Just some names are not gonna connect the dots for the cops. Why didn't you just give your info to the FBI?'

'Raggio,' I said. 'That asshole pissed me off. I don't wanna see him get any credit.'

'You'd rather give it to Hargrove?'

'In a heartbeat.'

'OK, then,' Jack said. 'Keep me clued in.'

I agreed, although I didn't know why. This part was really my problem. If Barney Irwin had tried to frame me for murder, I wanted his ass.

And I was gonna get it.

We got to my house before seven p.m. I pried my fingers from the dashboard, because Jerry had made it in record time.

When we got in the house Jerry said, 'So where's the note?'

'It was in my windbreaker,' I said. 'The one I wore that day.'

He followed me to the hall closet, where I grabbed the windbreaker from a hanger. I went through the pockets, found a couple of business cards, a restaurant receipt, a book of matches, all the crap you stuff into your pockets.

No note.

'It's gotta be here,' I said. I went through the pockets again.

'You sure this is the jacket you wore when we searched his place?' Jerry asked.

'Positive.'

'Well, I know you took it, because you showed it to me. So it's gotta be here someplace.'

We started to search. Kitchen drawers and cabinets; bathroom waste basket and counter, behind the bowl, under the sink; hall and bedroom, closets; beneath the cushions of the living-room chairs and sofa.

'Nothin',' I said, frustrated.

'We looked everywhere, Mr G. How about your locker at the Sands?'

'We can look, but I doubt it.'

'Then let's go.'

We left the house and went back out to the Caddy. It was getting dark and, suddenly, I got an idea.

'You got your pen light on ya?'

'Yep.'

'Let me have it.'

He passed it over. I clicked it on, shined it on the front seat. I stuck my hand between the back rest and the cushion on the passenger side, and then on the driver's side.

'Bingo,' I said, feeling something. I grabbed it between my index and middle finger and pulled. It was crumpled, but I smoothed it out and saw it was the piece of paper I'd found in Irwin's desk.

'There you go,' I said. 'Look.' I handed it over.

'Sinatra,' Jerry said, 'and Canoga Park.'

'That can't be a coincidence,' I argued. 'Also, Frankie said the kidnappers called each other by name. Joe. Barry. And John – or Johnny.'

'What about November twenty-second?' Jerry asked.

'The day JFK was shot.'

'You think this photographer was involved in the assassination?' he asked.

'No,' I said, 'I think he was either involved with or knew about the kidnapping.'

'What about Keenan and Amsler?'

'Could be last names to go with the first names we've got,' I said.

'So Barry Keenan or Barry Amsler? Or Joe Keenan, Joe Amsler? And what about the date?'

'Maybe,' I said. 'Maybe that was the original planned date of the kidnapping.'

'And when JFK got shot they called it off?'

I nodded.

'So whataya wanna do with this, Mr G.? Give it to that Hargrove asshole?'

'I'd rather give it to that asshole than Raggio. He's a bigger asshole. But before we do, let's see what Danny's found out. I'll call him to meet us.'

We went back inside.

FIFTY-THREE

I tried Danny at home first. When he didn't answer I called his office, not really expecting to find him there. I was surprised when he answered.

'I have some info,' he said. 'Let's meet.'

'OK,' I said. 'The Horseshoe. Fifteen minutes.'

Since he was down the street, he got there before us. We slid into the booth across from him.

'You fellas wanna order?' the waitress asked.

'Burger and fries,' Danny said. He looked at us. 'I haven't eaten today.'

'Burger and fries sounds good,' I said.

'Two,' Jerry said.

'Don't you mean three?' the waitress asked.

'No,' Jerry said, 'I mean I want two burgers, and a double order of fries.'

'OK,' she said, 'four hamburgers, four fries. Drinks?'

We all ordered Cokes. What was a burger without a Coke?

'Here's what I got—'

'Before you tell us, let me tell you what we got,' I said. 'Frank Jr. is home, the cops and the FBI are still looking for the kidnappers.'

'Frank Sr. must be relieved.'

'He is,' I said, 'but we rushed back here because of this.'

I pushed the crumpled piece of paper over to his side of the table. He smoothed it, read it.

'What's this?'

'Frankie says he was held in Canoga Park.'

Danny looked down at the note paper.

'Canoga Park,' he said. 'Sinatra. November twenty-second?'

'Mr G. thinks that might be the original date of the kidnapping.'

'And they called it off when JFK got shot,' Danny said, nodding. 'Makes sense. Amsler & Keenan? You know those names?'

'I don't,' I said.

'What about Barry, Joe, or Johnny?'

'Irwin's name is Barney, but I doubt he would've misspelled his own name.'

'Wait a minute,' Danny said. He took his note pad from his pocket, flipped a few pages. 'Here it is. Barney Irwin has a brother.' He looked at both of us. 'His name's John.'

'Johnny,' Jerry said.

If one of the kidnappers was John Irwin, then the others were either Barry Keenan and Joe Amsler, or Barry Amsler and Joe Keenan.

'Danny, do you have a lead on Barney Irwin's whereabouts?'

'I've checked his studio and his house again,' Danny said. 'He ain't been back.'

'Maybe he was with his brother and these other guys in Canoga Park,' I said.

'We've got to call somebody,' Danny said.

'Not that prick Raggio, the Washoe County DA,' I said.

'What about Hargrove?' Danny asked.

'That asshole!' Jerry said.

'Who's that leave?' Danny asked. 'The FBI?'

'If I could find the guy who saved my ass in Reno I'd give the info to him,' I said. 'Agent Kent.'

'What about the LA County DA?' Danny asked.

'Not as much of an ass,' I said.

'What about Frank?' Danny asked. 'We could give the info to him.'

'Frank's carryin' a gun, Danny,' I said. 'He might go off the deep end if he found these guys.'

'OK, not Frank. What about Entratter? What would he do with the information?'

We sat silent for a moment, then Jerry said, 'He might call Mo Mo.'

'And then those guys turn up dead,' Danny said.

'There's Frank's lawyer, Mickey Rudin,' I said. 'He seems on the level.'

'He does work for Frank, though.'

'I don't think he wants Frank on trial for murder,' I said.

'OK,' Danny said, 'OK, so you give the names to Mickey Rudin. He'll probably give them to the DA, or the FBI.'

'But the decision will be his,' I said.

'Frank's gonna be pissed you didn't tell him, Mr G.,' Jerry said.

'I'll have to take that chance, Jerry,' I said. 'I can't let Frank find these guys.'

'Eddie,' Danny said, 'we got names now. I could try and track these guys. We could pick them up ourselves.'

'It'll take a while,' I said. 'They might get away in the meantime. We need to plant this info somewhere it'll do the most good, so the cops and FBI can set up roadblocks and catch these guys. I'm not lookin' to play hero, Danny.'

'Then let's back track,' Danny said. 'Evans, the FBI, or Rudin. The decision is yours.'

I thought a moment, then said, 'OK, I'll go with Evans. He can mobilize both the LA cops and the FBI.'

'OK,' Danny said.

The waitress came with our food.

'I better get going,' I said.

'Mr G.,' Jerry whined, 'the food's here.'

'Take a half hour to eat, Eddie,' Danny said. 'You can call Evans after you finish.'

'Yeah, OK,' I said. 'Suddenly, I'm starvin'.'

'Me, too.' Jerry picked up one of his burgers.

'You?' Danny said. 'You're always starvin'.'

'I burn lots of calories.'

Danny and I stared at him.

'It's true,' he said. 'I learned about it from the Joe Franklin Show.'

FIFTY-FOUR

Rather than drive back to my house or the Sands, Danny suggested I call Evans in LA from his office. Jerry and I walked there with him. I sat at Penny's desk and made the call. It was after hours, but I got through to somebody at the DA's office and told them it concerned the Frank Sinatra Jr. kidnapping.

'I'm sorry, sir, Mr Evans isn't here at the moment.'

'I need to know where he is,' I said. 'I have information that could lead to the capture of the kidnappers. Can you give me his home number?'

'He's not home, either, sir. Why don't you give me your name and I'll have District Attorney Evans call you as soon as—'

I broke the connection and swore, 'Damn!'

'What happened?

'Evans isn't in his office and they say he's not home,' I said.

'Then where is he?' Danny asked.

I looked at Jerry and at the same time we said, 'Nancy's house.' Well, I said Nancy, he said 'Mrs S.'

I had the number of Nancy's house in my pocket. I called and the phone was answered by Ed Pucci.

'Ed, it's Eddie G., from Vegas.'

'Hey, Eddie. What's up?'

'Is Evans still there?'

'Yeah, he's across the room from me. Hold on.'

After a few seconds Evans came on the phone.

'What is it, Mr Gianelli?'

'I've got some information I think you should have, Mr Evans . . .'

I hung up and looked at Jerry and Danny.

'What'd he say?' Danny asked.

'He said "thank you".'

'Is he gonna tell Frank?' Danny asked.

'I don't know,' I said. 'He listened to me, I assume he took notes, then he thanked me and hung up.'

Danny laughed.

'What's so funny?'

'He's gonna catch those kidnappers, and take all the credit.'

'I don't really care,' I said, 'as long as they get caught.'

'Make sure you let Frank know it was you who gave Evans the information,' Danny said. 'Don't let him take the credit with him.'

'Yeah, OK.'

Danny looked at Jerry, and saw Jerry nod once. If I didn't tell Frank, the big guy would.

'What are we gonna do now?' Jerry asked.

'I'm gonna talk to Hargrove,' I said.

'What for?' Danny asked.

'To find out if they tracked down Wayne's killer,' I said. 'If they're still lookin' at me for it.'

'That Irwin guy wouldn't have the balls to do it himself,' Jerry said.

'Right. He sent those two guys to Reno to do me, and three to Brooklyn to do you,' I said. 'He's got the nerve for that, he had the nerve to have Wayne killed. And maybe Hargrove managed to identify them as the killers.'

'You walk into Hargrove's arms, he just might hang on to you,' Danny said.

'I'll take that chance,' I said. 'I didn't do anything, and he can't prove I did.'

'I'll go with you,' Jerry said.

'No chance,' I said. 'He sees you he'll throw you into a cell.'

'Don't go to his office,' Danny suggested. 'Have him meet you somewhere.'

I thought about it, then said, 'Yeah, OK. I'll have him meet me.'

'Us,' Jerry said.

I looked at Jerry, saw that he meant it.

'Yeah, OK, Jerry. Us.'

FIFTY-FIVE

To my surprise Hargrove agreed to meet. He picked the place, though. When we pulled up in front we realized what it was.

'A cop bar,' Jerry said.

'That's great.'

'Wanna shitcan it?' Jerry asked. 'Make him pick someplace else?'

I thought a moment. 'No, let's do it.'

We got out of the car and walked into the bar. I didn't know at the time if he had said anything to the others in the place, but it felt like they were all looking at us while we walked to the booth he was in. It reminded me of Clipper's, Irwin's hangout.

He was sitting alone, no partner. He looked as if he had come straight from work, still had on his suit, but no tie and his collar was open. It was probably the first time I'd ever seen him without a tie.

'You brought your friend,' he said. 'Good. I won't have to go lookin' for him. Have a seat.'

Jerry slid into the booth first, and I followed.

'Beer?'

'Sure.'

He waved at the bartender, held up three fingers. The man immediately came over and laid down three mugs.

'All these guys cops?' I asked, looking around.

'Cops, or ex-cops.'

'They know who we are?'

'No,' Hargrove said, 'but that don't mean they won't tear you apart if I say so.'

'And why would you do that?' I asked.

'I don't know,' Hargrove said. 'Why don't you tell me what you've got on your mind?'

I sipped my beer, made him wait.

'You find your killer yet?' I asked.

'Not yet. We did find a couple more witnesses, though.'

'Witnesses to what?'

'Two men – one your size, and one his –' he nodded at Jerry – 'seen around a photography studio on South Decatur, where our victim sometimes worked.'

'Worked? As what?'

'We don't know,' Hargrove said, 'we can't seem to find the photographer.'

'And I'll tell you why.'

I hadn't yet decided what I would tell him about how we came to find the slip of paper with all the names on it. But since I'd given the information to the Los Angeles DA already, I figured there'd be no harm giving it to Hargrove. After all, I still wanted to find Barney Irwin, and whoever killed Wayne. And if we could find the two knuckle-draggers who worked me over, even better.

'I just got back from LA, where I helped recover Frank Sinatra Jr. from his kidnappers.'

'Is that a fact?' Hargrove asked. 'You're a regular fuckin' hero, aren't you?'

'Yeah, he is,' Jerry said.

'Hey, it talks,' Hargrove said.

'Detective, why make him mad?' I asked. 'He could do a lot of damage in here.'

'And get his ass shot.'

'Be worth it,' Jerry said.

Hargrove stared at Jerry for a few moments, but the big guy never even blinked. The detective looked back at me.

'I can get a witness to ID both of you idiots in a heartbeat,' he said. 'Give me one reason why I shouldn't.'

'Because I don't wanna be a hero,' I said, 'but I can make you look like one.'

'How?'

This was where I took a chance. I brought the slip of paper out of my pocket and put it on the table.

'What's this?'

'Frank Jr. was kidnapped from Lake Tahoe and taken to Canoga Park,' I said, pointing to those words on the page. 'He said he was grabbed by three men named Barry, Joe and John – or Johnny. The photographer your victim, Wayne, worked for is named Barney Irwin. He has a brother named . . .' I tapped the name on the paper. '. . . Johnny.'

Hargrove looked at the paper again, this time more intently.

'You're telling me this photographer, Irwin, was involved in the kidnapping?'

'At the very least he knew about it,' I said. 'And his brother was involved.'

'What about this date? The twenty-second? The day JFK got hit.'

'I think that might have been the original date they were gonna grab Frankie. The assassination changed their minds.'

Hargrove picked the piece of paper up for the first time.

'Where did you get this?'

'If I tell you,' I said, carefully, 'I don't wanna get pinched.'

'Me neither,' Jerry said.

Hargrove chewed on the inside of his cheek for a few moments.

'If this leads me to my killer,' he said, 'and Irwin, and it turns out he was involved in the kidnapping, you guys are off the hook.'

'I got that out of Irwin's desk, in his studio.'

'What were you doin' there?'

'A favor for a friend.'

'After the murder?'

'Before,' I said, 'way before.'

'What was the favor?'

'That's not on the table,' I said.

'Gotta be discreet with your show-business friends, huh?'

'I don't wanna get arrested,' I said, 'and I don't wanna lose my job, either.'

'I'm gonna keep this,' he said, tapping the paper with his finger.

'Go ahead. I copied it.'

He put it in his pocket, drank some beer.

'If this pans out, I'll forget about breaking and entering and tampering with evidence,' he said. 'But I can't forget about murder, if you had anythin' to do with it.'

'We didn't,' I said. 'I guarantee it.'

Hargrove looked at Jerry.

'You,' he said, 'don't leave town.'

'Why would I?' Jerry asked. 'I love Vegas.'

'Yeah,' he said. 'Now get out of my bar. You're makin' me look bad.'

'One more thing.'

'What?'

I told him about the two torpedoes who worked me over in Reno. I didn't mention that Jerry had to kill three in Brooklyn.

'I think Irwin sent them after me.'

'Describe 'em.'

I did.

'Ring a bell?' I asked.

Hargrove sat back in his chair and regarded me for a moment.

'Sounds like the Rienza Brothers.'

'Italians?' Jerry asked.

'Working for Irwin,' I said.

'They work for anybody who'll pay the freight,' Hargrove said. 'OK, I'll look into them, too. Now will you leave?'

'We're gone,' I said.

'Remember,' he said, 'don't leave town.'

I paused getting out of the booth.

'Now what?'

'Might have to go to LA to see Frank,' I said. 'And the LA County DA wants to talk to me.' I was stretching the truth.

'Yeah, OK,' Hargrove said, 'if that happens, call me and let me know.'

'You got it.'

I slid out of the booth and Jerry followed me. As we walked to the door we were the center of attention, again. Or rather, Jerry was. My guess was they could always tell somebody who wasn't working the same side of the street as they were.

Outside Jerry said, 'Don't make me do that again, Mr G.'

'Do what?'

'Go in a cop bar.'

'Yeah,' I said, looking back at the door, 'let's neither one of us ever do that again.'

FIFTY-SIX

This time we drove back to the Sands. I got Jerry a room – 'A regular one,' he insisted – so he could spend the night comfortably. Then I went to see Jack Entratter in his office.

'What's goin' on?' he asked when I walked in. It wasn't a demand. In fact, he was sitting back in his chair and said it very nonchalantly.

I'd already explained it to DA Evans and Detective Hargrove, so giving it to Jack didn't take very long.

He thought the information over for a few moments, then said, 'You didn't tell Frank?'

'Jack, when we went out to deliver the money, Frank had a gun,' I said. 'I don't want him gettin' himself in trouble.'

'Guess you're right,' he said. 'If he got the chance he'd probably blow the heads off those scumbags.'

'So I told Evans, figured he'd act on it, then told Hargrove so he wouldn't throw me into a cell.'

'And I'm third on the totem pole, huh?'

'Don't get offended, Jack.'

'I'm not offended,' Entratter said, wearily. 'I'm tired. This whole Frankie thing . . . if the kidnappers get caught, then I'm glad you told whoever you told. Now, what's happening here, in Vegas, that's gonna keep you from workin'?'

'Nothing,' I said. 'I mean, hopefully, when they catch the kidnappers, everything else will go away.'

'So whatever you stirred up when you were helping Abby will be over, too?'

'I said . . . hopefully.'

'Yeah . . . take tonight off, Eddie. See you at work tomorrow.'

'OK.'

As I stood up he said, 'Oh, wait.'

'Yeah?'

'What about Jerry? Where is he?'

'I stuck him in a room,' I said. 'A regular, normal room.'

'Is he goin' home tomorrow?'

'He's gonna stick around,' I said. 'Um, Hargrove kinda told him to stick around until everything is . . . resolved.'

'Resolved,' Jack said. 'That's a good word.'

'Yeah.'

'Tell me, what's gonna happen when they catch the kidnappers in LA and Hargrove realizes you gave them the info before you gave it to him?'

'I don't know,' I said. 'I guess I'll have to deal with that when the time comes.'

'Get some sleep, Eddie,' he said. 'You look like shit.'

I went home.

Jack was right. I was exhausted. I fell on to my bed without getting undressed and when I opened my eyes, it was morning. Not early morning. It was ten. Jerry had probably had pancakes by now. That was good. I wasn't quite up to watching him work his way through two stacks.

I showered, got dressed, made myself a simple egg sandwich for breakfast, washed it down with coffee while I watched the TV. Frankie's return home was a big story. Also, the fact that the kidnappers were still on the loose, and were being hunted. The police said that their capture 'was imminent.' I wondered if that was because of my information.

I was getting dressed when the phone rang.

'Hello?'

'We gotta talk,' a man said.

'If I knew who you were—'

'It's Irwin,' he said. 'We gotta talk.'

'About what?'

'I can help you.'

'Help me do what?'

'Catch my brother, and his two idiot friends.'

'Amsler and Keenan?'

He hesitated. I could hear him breathing on the other end.

'You know more than I thought.'

'I know about Canoga Park, I even know about November twenty-second.'

'Yeah,' Irwin said, 'they was gonna grab the kid that day. The JFK thing shit-canned all that.'

'So where are they?'

'Ya gotta meet me,' Irwin said. 'And I need some money. You shorted me last time.'

'Why would I give you money?'

'I gotta get away.'

'Seems to me you've done a pretty good job of going underground.'

'I been in LA, but I came back.'

'Why?'

'To pack my stuff,' Irwin said. 'This time when I disappear I want it to be for good.'

'I don't have any money, Barney.'

'You must have . . . some.'

'I can probably scrape together a couple of thousand.'

'That's all?'

'If you wanted more you should've stuck with your brother and got your cut.'

'No, it wasn't like that,' he said. 'I wasn't involved, nor that I should get a cut.'

'Two grand, Barney,' I said. 'That's it.'

Again, he breathed heavily into the phone.

'Yeah, yeah, OK,' he said. 'Two thousand.'

'Where do you want to meet?'

'You know that warehouse you and your big goon took me to?'

'Yeah.'

'We'll meet there.'

'When?'

'In an hour.'

'An hour?'

'Yeah, I don't wanna give you too much time to . . . get some help.'

'Why would I need help to pay you for some information, Barney?'

'I'm . . . just sayin'.'

'OK, Barney,' I said, 'the warehouse in an hour.'

'Don't forget the two grand.'

'I've got just enough time to go to the bank and get it.'

'That's what I figured,' he said, and hung up.

I called Jerry.

'It's a set up,' he said.

'That's what I was thinking,' I said. 'By giving me an hour, he figures I don't have time to fly you in.'

'Unlucky for him I'm already here,' Jerry said. 'And two grand? I don't think Irwin would cross the street for that kinda dough, Mr G.'

'Again,' I said, 'we're thinkin' alike. He doesn't seem to be any smarter than his brother and friends. They only asked for two hundred and forty grand from Frank.'

'They're all stupid amateurs,' Jerry said.

'I'm comin' to get you, Jerry,' I said, 'and then we'll hit the warehouse.'

'OK, Mr G. I'll be out front.'

I hung up, grabbed my jacket and keys and was out the door.

FIFTY-SEVEN

I swung up in front of the Sands, waved through by the valets, who recognized me. Jerry jumped into the passenger seat and I took off again.

'Did you get the two grand?' he asked.

'No,' I said, 'since we don't intend to pay him, I didn't bother.'

He showed me a brown envelope. 'I put some brochures inside.' It looked like it was thick with money. 'Just in case.'

'Good thinkin', Jerry.'

We drove downtown to the warehouse where Jerry thought he had succeeded in scaring Barney Irwin half to death.

'I don't get it,' Jerry said. 'If he's got money from the kidnappin' why would he bother to come back here? Why not get lost?'

'Maybe it's worth it to him to get back at me,' I said.

'That's what I mean,' Jerry said. 'Amateurs. He shoulda just forgot about it and took off.'

'He claims he didn't get a cut from the kidnapping,' I said. 'If that's true it could explain why he's back, but it doesn't explain why he'd settle for only two grand.'

When we pulled up to the warehouse there were no other vehicles around.

'Might be around back,' Jerry said.

I started the car again and rode around the building. No cars, no trucks. Once again I stopped near the front door.

'You got a gun?'

'A forty-five.'

We walked to the door and tried it, found it unlocked. The inside was dark. There seemed to be a single bulb burning somewhere in the center. Probably the one that had been hanging over Irwin's head last time.

I could barely see Jerry but he gave me some hand signals which I assumed meant he was going to lay back in the dark. I nodded. He handed me the envelope full of brochures.

I advanced toward the light. The chair Irwin had been sitting in was still there. This seemed more and more like a trap, Irwin looking for payback, either because he was still afraid of Jerry, or because I was the one who put him in that chair with Jerry.

'Barney!' I called. My voice echoed in the empty warehouse interior. 'Come on, Barney.'

There was a moment of silence, then a voice said, 'Come to the center of the room. I wanna make sure you're alone.'

If he had gotten there first – which he obviously had – he was pretty dumb if he hadn't been watching the parking lot to see if I would come alone.

I walked, eventually entering the small circle of light thrown by the naked bulb.

'You got the money?' the voice asked. It sounded like Irwin, but I couldn't really tell.

'I've got it.'

'Put it on the chair.'

I walked to the chair, laid the envelope down, then stepped back.

'Come on, Barney, stop playin' games. I'm not just gonna leave this on the chair. Come on out.'

'I ain't so sure I wanna come out,' Irwin said.

'Barney, come on . . . what's this all about. Why'd you call the cops and tell them I killed your friend Wayne?'

There was a pause, then he said, 'Somebody killed Wayne?'

'Yeah, well, I figured it was you, and you were tryin' to jam me up with the cops by givin' them my name.'

No reply.

'It didn't work. I'm still walkin' around free.'

'You had no right,' he said, finally.

'No right to do what?'

'What you did to me,' Irwin said. 'You ruined my business, you left me alone with that . . . that animal, and then you short changed me.'

'Barney, I don't think I ruined your business, I think I put it out of its misery. As far as leavin' you alone with Jerry, that was your own fault. And finally, you got more money than you deserved.'

Again, silence.

I heard the sound of feet scraping on the concrete floor. I hoped it wasn't Jerry. Then again, maybe it would have been better if it was Jerry. As it was, two figures stepped into the circle of light, coming from different directions. It was the Rienza brothers, my old buddies from Reno.

FIFTY-EIGHT

'Not so smart, are ya?' one asked.

'You don't learn your lesson, do ya?' the other asked.

'Actually,' I said, 'I do.'

'Huh?' one asked.

Their huge hands were empty, no guns, so when Jerry stepped out of the dark, his gun was still tucked away.

'Meet my friend,' I said.

The two of them eyed Jerry warily. They were big, but he was bigger. In the darkness I heard some more feet scraping the floor, and then the sound of running. At the sight of Jerry, Irwin was taking off.

'Hey,' one of the Rienzas said, 'he ain't supposed to be here.'

'Go, Mr G.,' Jerry said. 'I got this.'

No weapons came out. It looked as if the Rienza brothers were gonna go *mano-a-mano* with Jerry. I wasn't sure about leaving him alone, but then I wasn't so sure I wouldn't be more hindrance to him than help if I stayed.

'Go!' he snapped.

At that moment a door opened somewhere in the warehouse. Light flooded in, and then the door slammed.

I turned and headed for the front door.

By the time I got outside there was no way I could figure out which door Irwin had used. I scanned the parking lot, but didn't see anyone running away from the place. Suddenly I heard the sound of a motor. From the left side of the warehouse a motorcycle appeared, heading for the street. The rider was wearing a helmet. The only way I knew it was Barney Irwin was the flash of pastels as he went by. Even the helmet was powder blue.

I thought about jumping in my car and chasing him, but I knew I'd never catch him. He was gone. We'd been looking for cars or trucks when we drove around the building. Somehow, we'd missed the bike.

I turned and went back inside.

In the circle of light Jerry had one of the Rienza brothers down on his belly. His hands were locked with the other one, as if they were in the center of a wrestling ring, and the Rienza was not faring well in the test of strength. His knees began to bend as Jerry slowly showed his superior strength.

The Rienza who was down was not out. He started to move and in the yellow light I saw a glint of metal. I ran forward and, for want of a better idea, I kicked the Rienza in the head. He grunted, dropped his gun to the concrete with a clatter.

'Gun, Jerry!' I said.

Jerry risked a look over his shoulder at me, then turned his attention back to the second Rienza. Abruptly, he lifted his knee into the man's face. I heard bones crunch and, as teeth fell to the floor, the other man fell on to his back with a groan. Jerry quickly bent, patted him down, and came away with a .38.

I picked up the first man's gun, which was also a .38.

'What about Irwin?' Jerry asked.

'He took off on a motorcycle by the time I got outside.'

'How did we miss that?'

I shrugged.

'How was that fella Wayne killed?' Jerry asked me. He wasn't even out of breath.

'I'm not sure.'

'Well,' he said, 'if he was shot, it might've been with one of these guns. These guys are dumb enough to keep it.'

I looked down at the two unconscious brothers.

'Maybe,' I said, 'we should make an anonymous call of our own to the cops.'

FIFTY-NINE

There were dumpsters behind the building. We found two more motorcycles behind them. That explained how we missed the Rienzas.

We found rope in my trunk and tied the brothers up before we left. Jerry unloaded their guns, and tossed them on the floor.

Jerry drove while I looked for a phone booth. He stayed in the car as I dialed and then made my anonymous call to the cops, giving them the address of the warehouse, saying I had heard shots.

I got back in the car.

'OK,' I said, 'later we'll have somebody call and drop Wayne's name. For now those two idiots will just be taken in and checked out. Hargrove won't let them go easily.'

'So where to now?' he asked.

'Back to the Sands, I guess.' The Sands seemed to be where it always started and ended for me. It was more home than home was.

When we got to the casino I was approached as soon as we walked into the lobby.

'Mr Entratter's lookin for you,' a bellman told me. 'Wants you in his office pronto.'

'OK, thanks.'

'I'll go to my room,' Jerry said.

'No, Come with me,' I said. 'Let's see what this is about.'

We took the elevator up. Jack's girl was back and, probably in deference to the fact that Jerry was with me, said, 'Go right in.'

As we entered Jack jumped up from behind his desk. 'They got the bastards!'

'The kidnappers?'

'Yep,' Entratter said. 'You were right, Eddie. The first one they caught was Johnny Irwin. He had forty grand with him. And then he gave up the other two.' He looked at a piece of paper on his desk. 'Joe Amsler and Barry Keenan.'

'You nailed that one, Mr G.,' Jerry said.

'You sure did,' Jack said. 'Frank wants you to come back to LA with me. You, too, Jerry. It's his birthday and he's havin' a party.'

'Today?'

'Right now,' Jack said. 'I was waitin' for you to show up so we could leave.'

'Um . . .'

'What's wrong?'

'I had a talk with Hargrove last night,' I said. 'He said if I had to go back to LA to let him know.'

'Well, OK,' Entratter said. 'Use my phone and let's get goin'.'

He moved around his desk so I could sit in his chair and call. It took a while for Hargrove to come to the phone, and when he did he sounded breathless.

'Who is it?'

'Eddie G.,' I said. 'I've got to go to LA. You wanted me to—'

'What are you tryin' to pull, Eddie?' he demanded.

Uh-oh, I thought, he'd already heard about the kidnappers.

'What do you mean?'

'What do I mean? I mean the Rienza brothers were found tied up in a warehouse downtown. Their guns were on the ground next to 'em, unloaded. You don't know anythin' about this, do you?'

'Why would I?' I asked. 'Did they say I did? Did anybody say I did?'

'They ain't talkin',' Hargrove said. 'What's goin' on in LA?'

'I don't know,' I lied. 'Frank told me to come back. He says he's got some news.'

'Well . . . fine. You go, but the minute you get back, haul your ass in here. I want to get to the bottom of this.'

'We still talkin' about the murder?' I asked. 'Did those two kill Wayne?'

'We're doing a ballistics check on their guns right now,' Hargrove said. 'By the time you get back, I'll know something.'

'OK, then,' I said. 'I'll see you when I get back.'

'You and your big friend aren't off the hook yet, Eddie,' he said. 'Get that idea out of your head.'

'Yes, Detective.'

'And make sure he comes in with you.'

'Yes, Detective.'

'Are you yessing me, Eddie?' he demanded. 'You think you're handling me, right now?'

I said, 'Yes, Detective,' and hung up.

SIXTY

Frank had called Chasen's and had them bring in enough food for an army. He invited Dean and Joey (Sammy was away doing a show) and all the FBI agents and cops who had worked on getting Frankie back. Also there when we arrived were Jimmy Van Heusen, Gloria and Mike Romanoff and a man I knew was his neighbor in Palm Springs, Abe Lipsey.

Van Heusen was a hugely successful songwriter who had written many of Frank's hits.

Gloria and Mike Romanoff owned one of the most popular restaurants in Hollywood, Romanoff's.

Lipsey was simply a rich neighbor who had no connections to Hollywood, except that he enjoyed hosting parties to which he invited both movie and television stars, mostly at his Sunset Boulevard mansion. The parties became so famous that invitations were much sought after.

The party was as much for Frankie as it was for Frank's birthday, but Nancy kept her son close to her during the entire proceedings, and she couldn't be blamed for that.

Frank was a cheerful host, telling anyone who would listen that getting Frankie back was the biggest and best birthday present he could ever have gotten.

At one point he cornered Entratter and me and started telling us how much he appreciated the police and the FBI.

'I'm gonna send each and every one of them somethin' special,' he said, 'as soon as I figure out what it should be. And you.' He grabbed me, put his arm around my neck and hugged me to him. 'You're gonna get the most special gift of all!'

'I don't need a gift, Frank,' I said. 'I'm just glad Frankie's home.'

'That's what I love about this guy,' he said to Jack, tightening his arm around my neck, 'he's modest. He's done more than anyone over the past few years to keep us bums out of trouble. Now he not only saves my son, but supplies the information that the cops used to catch the kidnappers – and he don't want nothin'.' He looked around. 'I need another drink.'

He went off to get one, got waylaid by Mike and Gloria Romanoff, kissed Gloria soundly before continuing on.

'Whatever he gives you,' Jack said, 'just say thank you, Eddie.'

'Jack—'

'He's comin' to Vegas tonight. Tomorrow we celebrate the Sands' eleventh anniversary, and he wants to be there. He's gonna bring Juliet Prowse with him.'

I'd forgotten about the anniversary party.

'But this will go on for a while,' Jack said, putting his hand on my shoulder. 'And you had a big part in bringin' Frankie home, and finding the kidnappers. So enjoy the celebration.'

I nodded, and Jack moved off to join Jilly Rizzo and Mickey Rudin in a corner.

Sometime later I found myself standing off to one side talking with Nancy and Tina Sinatra. Or maybe we were flirting. We'd all had a lot to drink and were relieved that Frankie was safe.

Nancy was hanging on to one of my arms and Tina the other when Frank came stalking over and stood in front of us.

'I love ya, Eddie . . .' he said.

'I love you, too, Frank.'

'. . . but stay away from my daughters!'

Both girls laughed as Frank grabbed me by the front of my shirt and pulled me away from them.

'Eddie, those girls ain't ready for you. You're Eddie G., slick, fast—'

'Slick?'

'Trustworthy and loyal.'

Like a boy scout? I thought.

'I love ya, pally,' he said again, slapping me lightly on the cheek, 'but those are my babies, ya know?'

'I know, Frank.'

He threw his arm around me again and said, 'Now if you want a broad, I can get ya a broad.'

'No, I'm good, Frank,' I said. 'Really.'

'OK.'

He walked away and I decided not to go back to the Sinatra girls. Besides, when I turned around they had latched on to a handsome young FBI agent, who was looking mortified.

Later I came face to face with Jimmy Van Heusen and found myself gushing to him about how much I enjoyed his work with Frank, including 'All the Way' and 'High Hopes', both of which won Oscars. He told me one of his favorite songs was 'Call Me Irresponsible' from that year's film *Papa's Delicate Condition.* I hadn't seen the film yet, but I heard the song on the radio by Jack Jones. He then told me something I didn't know, that he originally wrote the song for Fred Astaire to sing in the movie, but Astaire had to pull out because of other obligations, so Jackie Gleason stepped in and did the film.

'It's on Frank's new album, though, "Sinatra's Sinatra",' he finished.

Somebody came and grabbed his arm, so I moved away after wishing him luck with the song at the next Oscar ceremony.

I looked around, saw Jerry standing off to one side eating a huge sandwich. He had a lot of room around him, like people were giving him space. I walked over and joined him. The table there was laden with food, both hot and cold.

'How you doin', big guy?'

'Good, Mr G. The food's real good. That Chasen's place must be OK.'

'I think so.'

Even though the food on the table was delicious I found I wasn't that hungry.

'*Manga*,' Jerry said.

'Maybe later. I'm gonna get another drink.'

I looked around and saw Evans walking up to me. He was holding two drinks.

'You look thirsty,' he said, handing me one.

'Thanks. You're a mind reader.' I sipped it. It was bourbon.

'Look, can we talk? Privately?'

'I'll see you later, Jerry,' I said.

He nodded, raised his sandwich, and chewed.

SIXTY-ONE

Evans and I found a corner where we could talk.

'I wanted to thank you again for the information you called me with,' Evans said. 'It really accelerated the capture of those kidnappers.'

'Accelerated?' I asked.

'Well, yes,' Evans said. He was impeccably decked out in an expensive brown suit with creases in his trousers that could carve a turkey and a burgundy pocket handkerchief. He wore gold cuff links, a couple of gold rings, but nothing on his wedding ring finger. I bet myself that he was always in the society pages, one of LA's most eligible bachelors. 'We were going to catch them, anyway. But you helped speed up the process.'

'I see.'

'So I don't think I should be reading anything in the newspapers about you being the one who caught the kidnappers.'

'Is that what you're worried about, Mr DA?' I asked. 'That I'm gonna try and take credit for bringin' Frankie home? And findin' the kidnappers?'

'Well, aren't you?'

'I don't care about the credit, Evans,' I said. 'You can have it.'

'You getting paid that much that you don't need to be the hero?'

'I'm not gettin' paid anythin'.'

He took a step back regarded me, puzzled.

'So you did this – all of this – for nothin'? For . . . what? Friendship?'

'That's right, friendship,' I said. 'Frank called and asked me to help, and I said yes.'

'And you put your life on the line?'

I shrugged.

'I don't understand that,' he said.

'What? The concept of someone doin' somethin' for a reason other than profit?'

'I'm a politician, Eddie,' he said. 'Altruism is not something I see every day. It's not something I even understand.'

I wasn't sure I knew what 'altruism' meant back then, but I pretty much figured it out.

'Some people just do the right thing, Mr Evans,' I said. 'And I guess that's somethin' I wouldn't expect a politician to get.'

For some reason he decided to take offense at that moment.

'Oh, look here,' he said, 'don't go getting so high and mighty on me. According to Mr Raggio you're nothin' but another hood. You work for the mob in one of their casinos, and you work to keep their friends out of trouble.'

'I think I'm done talking to you, Mr Evans,' I said. 'I see a lot more interesting people in the room.'

'Yeah, you listen—'

'Dino!' I yelled.

Dean Martin had just walked in. He spotted me and came walking over.

'Hey, Eddie!' He gave me a big hug. 'Who do we have here?'

'This is Mr Evans, the District Attorney around here. He worked with the cops and the FBI on gettin' Frankie back.'

'Well,' Dino said to Evans, 'let me shake your hand, fella. You did a helluva job.'

Evans shook hands with Dean but studied me. I guess he was waiting for me to play hero.

'Thank you, Mr Martin,' he said. 'I was just . . . just doing my job.'

Dino looked at me, a smile on his handsome face. He was wearing a blue suit that made the DA's look cheap.

'I wanted to come over while everything was going on, but Frank said no. He said it would attract too much attention.'

'He was quite right,' Evans said. 'We had enough media attention to deal with.'

'Well,' Dean said, 'it's a pleasure to meet you. Eddie, I'll see you later. I'm gonna go and find Frank and Frankie, so I can give the kid a big hug. Excuse me boys.'

'Yes, sir,' Evans said.

I nodded and Dean moved away into the room crowded with Sinatra well wishers.

I caught Evans looking at me.

'Maybe I misjudged you, Eddie,' he said, finally.

'You know what, Evans?' I said. 'It really doesn't matter whether you did or didn't because we probably won't ever see each other again after this.'

'You're right,' Evans said. 'We probably won't.'

He turned and followed in Dino's wake into the crowded room.

SIXTY-TWO

We got off Frank's plane the next morning in Vegas and found the cops waiting for us.

'What's this about?' Entratter said aloud as we came down the airstairs.

Frank had Juliet Prowse on his arm, put himself between her and the advancing quartet of uniformed cops.

'Take it easy, baby,' he told her.

'Eddie Gianelli?' one of them asked as they reached us.

'That's me.'

'You're comin' with us,' he said.

'Am I?'

'Under your own power or by force, but yeah, you're comin',' he said.

'Why?'

'Detective Hargrove wants to see you.'

'Uh-oh,' Entratter said.

I knew what he meant. Hargrove had heard about the capture of the kidnappers and he knew that I gave him the information second, not first.

Mickey Rudin came out of the plane and asked, 'What's going on?'

'I think Eddie needs a lawyer, Mickey,' Frank said. 'These officers are taking him in. I want you to go with him.'

'What's this about?' Rudin asked anybody who would answer.

'It has to do with a murder investigation,' the cops said. 'That's all I can say right now, sir.'

'I'm Mr Gianelli's lawyer.'

'Then you might as well come with us,' the cop said.

'All right,' Rudin said, wearily. He looked at Frank.

'We'll take your bags to the Sands,' Frank said. 'Meet you there.' Then he looked at me. 'Both of you.'

'OK,' Rudin said.

'Thanks, Frank,' I said.

'Mickey will bring you home,' Frank said. 'Don't worry.' Juliet gave me a dazzling smile of encouragement over Frank's shoulder.

'OK, boys,' I said, extending my wrists, 'take me to your leader.'

'There won't be any need for cuffs, Mr Gianelli,' the cops said. 'We have a car over here.'

I fell into step with two of them. The other two walked behind us.

Back in the same interview room. I could tell because the wall clock had a paint smudge on it, probably from the last time the room was painted.

Hargrove was going to be mad. I knew that. When he saw the news last night, or that morning, he must have hit the roof. He had the cops watching the airport for Frank's plane, figured I'd be coming back. Now I was going to be back on the stove for the murder of Wayne Whatsisname.

When he came in I was braced for him to be yelling and screaming, red in the face. Instead the door opened and he walked in, all calm and collected. He took off his jacket, hung it over the back of a chair, then sat down at the table across from me. He took the time to light a cigarette, and then rolled up the sleeves of his white shirt.

'You fucked me, Eddie.'

'Did I?'

'That information you gave me was old,' he said. 'Probably only hours old, but old enough for the LA cops to make the pinch.'

'But that's good, right?' I asked. 'They caught the kidnappers.'

'Yeah, that's good,' Hargrove said, 'that's real good . . . for them. But I didn't have anything to do with it. So you know what that means?'

'What?'

'You're back on the hook for Wayne's murder. You and your big buddy. Where is he, anyway? He wasn't on the plane with you. I told you guys not to leave town for long.'

'He'll be back later this afternoon, on a commercial flight.'

'That's good, that's real good.'

'What about the Rienza brothers?' I asked. 'Are you still holdin' 'em, or did you let 'em go?'

'Those two idiots are still in a cell,' he said. 'One of their guns came up as being used in a robbery in LA. We're still checking on the other one.'

'How do they look for Wayne?'

'They have alibis,' Hargrove said, 'but we're still checking those out.'

'How come you never asked me for my alibi?'

'Because I knew you'd have one. Probably unbreakable. That wouldn't mean you didn't do it.'

'Wow,' I said. 'That's quite an attitude for a detective to take. That could apply to anyone.'

'Not everyone has your friends, Eddie. For instance, you got a hotshot lawyer outside, makin' all kinds of noise about wanting me to let you go.'

'Mickey Rudin.'

'Yeah, Sinatra's mouthpiece, right?'

'That's right.'

'That means you ain't gonna call your buddies, the Kennedys, to get you out this time?'

That had happened some time ago, and it obviously still stuck in his craw.

'No,' I said, 'it means you're gonna bust my balls for a while and then let me go.'

'Why would I do that?'

'Which one? Bust my balls, or let me go?'

'Both,' Hargrove said, 'in any order you like.'

'Well, you'll bust my balls because you're a sonofabitch, but you'll let me go because you're a good detective.'

He seemed to be surprised by one of those statements.

'Eddie, Eddie . . .'

'I didn't kill Wayne Whatsisname, Detective,' I said, 'and neither did Jerry. Let me out of here and I'll prove it.'

'Now you're a detective?'

'You're the detective,' I said. 'Let's just call me the assistant detective.'

He studied me for a moment.

'Whataya say?'

SIXTY-THREE

Forty-eight hours.

That's what Hargrove gave me. When they were gone he said he'd be bringing me and Jerry in for some line-ups.

I rode back to the Sands with Mickey Rudin in a car Jack Entratter had sent.

'Thanks for comin' along, Mr Rudin,' I said.

'Mickey, please,' Rudin said. 'I don't think Detective Hargrove will be bothering you anymore, Eddie. If he does, just give me a call.'

I studied Rudin's profile, because he didn't look at me when he spoke. I was sure he thought his presence had gotten me sprung, but the fact was I had gotten myself out. Since Frank was nice enough to send his lawyer with me, though, I didn't do anything to disappoint him.

When we got to the Sands I took Mickey to the front desk to get him the key to his suite. He went upstairs to freshen up, once more assuring me that he was at my disposal.

When he was gone I called Jerry's room. I had lied to Hargrove. Jerry was on Frank's plane, but when he saw the uniformed cops coming, he chose to stay behind until they left – with me in tow.

'Hey, Mr G.,' he said. 'That was fast.'

'Believe it or not, Hargrove was reasonable,' I said.

'What did you promise him?'

'The killer of good ol' Wayne.'

'How we gonna find that out?'

'You and me,' I said, 'are gonna find Barney Irwin.'

'How?'

'This is my town, Jerry,' I said. 'I'm gonna pull out all the stops.'

'This I gotta see, Mr G.'

'Well, meet me in the lobby,' I said, 'and be ready to drive.'

My contacts in town were extensive.

Before JFK's death I had put the word out to some of my people, but I'd never really had a chance to cash in. The assassination had taken up most of their time and attention.

This time around, I was gonna hit everybody, and stay on their asses.

We made the rounds on the strip of valets, car hops, bellmen and doormen and waitresses, not to mention the maitre d's.

After that I directed Jerry to drive off the strip. Every few blocks I had him pull over so I could talk to a vendor, a street performer, a cabbie, a truck driver. I had him wait outside buildings while I talked to reporters, photographers, doormen, security guards, reporters; people I knew had their own ears on the streets.

'Now what?' he asked, when I hopped back into the car after talking to a waitress at a downtown restaurant.

'Now we're really gonna get down and dirty,' I said. 'Drive.'

I directed him to a part of town he felt very comfortable in.

'Now these are my people,' he said, looking at the hookers and stoners.

'Down boy,' I said. 'You're a lot better than this.'

'Thanks, Mr G.,' he said, 'but sometimes I ain't so sure.'

I directed him down a side street and immediately a couple of girls approached the car, one on each side.

'Wow,' one girl said to him, 'you're a big one.' She was a blowsy blonde with big breasts squeezed into a top two sizes too small.

'Call off your friend, Darla,' I said to the skinnier brunette on my side.

'Back off, Candy,' Darla said. 'Eddie here is a friend of mine, not a client.'

'What about you, sugar?' Candy said to Jerry. 'Wanna do some business?'

'Not right now, thanks, baby,' he said. As tongue tied as Jerry was around Ava Gardner and Abby Dalton, he knew how to talk to hookers. 'Maybe some other time.'

'What's on your mind, Eddie?' Darla asked.

'I'm lookin' for a guy who's probably hidin' out,' I said. 'A photographer named Barney Irwin.'

'I know Barney,' she said. 'He's a sleazeball, always tryin' to get me to strip for his camera.'

'He hasn't succeeded?'

'I don't do nothin' for nothin', Eddie, you know that.'

'I do know that.' I handed her a twenty. 'Keep an eye out, put the word out. A C-note for anybody who finds him and lets me know.'

'You got it, handsome.'

The double sawbuck disappeared into her bra.

'Bye, sweetie,' Darla said to Jerry.

'So long.'

'Your friend knows where to find my friend, if you get the time,' she said.

'I'll remember.'

Jerry put the car in drive and I directed him up a few more blocks.

'Pull over here.'

He pulled to the curb and stopped.

'What's here?'

'Wait for it.'

We waited a few minutes and then a guy came staggering down the street. When he got to the car he sort of lurched, bounced off the hood and ended up by my door.

'Hey, Eddie.'

'Dewey.'

'You're not lookin' ta score, so what's up?'

I told him what I told Darla. He didn't know Irwin, but took his description and promised to be on the lookout, and pass the word. After that he staggered off.

'I hate stoners,' Jerry said.

'He's not a stoner,' I said. 'He's a dealer. Never uses his own stuff, just acts like it.'

'Don't like dealers, either.'

'Well, you don't have to deal with him, I do.'

'Where to?' Jerry asked. 'Time to eat?'

'Yeah, but not around here. Drive. I'll tell you where.'

SIXTY-FOUR

I asked Jerry if he wanted hot dogs but he said not unless they were from Nathan's of Nedicks. We settled on burgers and I directed him to a small burger shack I'd never taken him to before.

'For a guy who'll eat anythin' you're a real hot dog snob,' I said to him when we sat down at an outdoor table with baskets of burgers and fries.

'Ain't my fault,' he said, with a shrug. 'Stuff in Brooklyn is real good. Come on, Mr G. Pizza? You got good pizza out here?'

I had to admit, Brooklyn pizza was still the best I'd ever had.

'We gonna call the dick today?'

'Yeah,' I said, 'right after this. He doesn't have as many ears on the street as I do, but he's got a network.'

'You know a helluva lot of people, Mr G.,' Jerry said. 'This photographer ain't got a chance of stayin' hid – unless he left town.'

'Even then we might be able to find out where he went.'

'What about hired help?' Jerry asked. 'If he hired them two jamokes at the warehouse he could hire some more.'

'Cheap labor,' I said. 'He either can't or won't lay out the dough for prime help.'

'That's good for us,' Jerry said. 'I'm gettin' another burger. Want one?'

'I'm still workin' on this one,' I said. 'I don't inhale food the way you do.'

He went off and came back with not only another burger, but another basket of fries. I still had half mine left. We were washing everything down with Cokes.

'Got any more people to hit today?' he asked. 'Some real lowlifes?'

'You don't think we talked to any lowlifes today?'

'That Dewey looked like a scumbag.'

'Not Candy and Darla?'

'They're just whores, Mr G.,' he said. 'Whores are OK. They're just workin' girls.'

'Well,' I said, 'we could go out to some of the ranches.'

'What ranches?' Jerry asked. 'We gonna talk to cowboys?'

'Brothels, Jerry,' I said. 'Whorehouses.'

'You call them ranches? Are they legal?'

'No, but they should be,' I said. 'Someday they will be, when the politicians get their heads out of their asses.'

'So they makin' payoffs?'

'Oh, yeah,' I said. 'They pay through the nose to operate.'

'You think Irwin went to one of 'em?'

'Not if he's cheap,' I said. 'Rather than go out there, I'll just make some calls.'

We finished eating and I went to a nearby pay phone to call Danny. I found him in his office, answering his own phone,

'Where's Penny?'

'Out. What's up?'

I told him I was spreading the word on Irwin, and wanted him to do the same.

'He may be on a bike.'

'A bike? Like a Schwinn?'

'No, like a Harley.'

'Irwin?'

'Last time I saw him.' I told him about the warehouse.

'You let him get away?'

'Don't rub it in,' I said.

'What about Jerry?'

'He was dancing with the Rienza brothers at the time.'

'The guys who jumped you in Reno?' he asked. 'Where are they now?'

'In jail. Hargrove's keepin' 'em under wraps.'

'How do you stand with him now?'

I explained how he'd taken me from the plane to an interview room, where we talked.

'Like human beings?'

'Believe it or not,' I said, 'we came to an understanding.'

'I don't believe it,' he said.

'I think he still sees a chance to get in on the kidnapping,' I said. 'Like catching the last one.'

'Barney Irwin?'

'Well, he's related to one of 'em,' I said. 'That's close enough for Hargrove.'

'OK, so I'll put the word out on Irwin,' he said. 'Between you and me we got the town wired. We'll find the bastard.'

'Call me when you do.'

'You do the same.'

We agreed and hung up. When I got back to the table I couldn't believe Jerry had another basket of fries.

'What the fuck?' I said.

'I got lonely.'

SIXTY-FIVE

When we got back to the Sands, Entratter had once again put the word out that he wanted to see me.

'Where is he?' I asked the bellman. 'In his office?'

'No, sir, I just saw him go out on the casino floor.'

'OK, thanks.'

'I'm gonna go to my room and wash up,' Jerry said. 'I'll meet ya out there.'

'OK.'

We split up and I went looking for Entratter. I found him watching two middle-aged women playing blackjack at a high stakes table.

'They're cleanin' up, and I can't figure out how,' he said.

'Maybe they're lucky.'

'Gotta be more than luck.'

'You wanted to see me,' I reminded him.

'You didn't come see me when you got back.'

'I figured Mickey would tell you what happened.'

'Mickey doesn't know what happened,' he said. 'He thinks he got you out just by bein' there.'

'You don't think he did?'

'Mickey's a good guy, but he gets a little puffed up about himself,' Entratter said. 'He ain't no criminal attorney.'

'No, he's not.'

'So what happened?'

'You wanna get a drink?'

'No,' Entratter said, 'I'm watchin' these two broads. Tell me here.'

'Hargrove and I came to an understanding.'

'How the hell did that happen?'

'He still thinks Barney Irwin had a hand in the kidnappin', and if he catches him, he cashes in on some of the glory.'

'And you let him think that?'

'Why not? What can it hurt? I'm thinkin' Irwin had somethin' to do with his man Wayne's murder. So I help Hargrove catch him, he charges him with the killin' and the kidnappin'. Where's the harm?'

'And how are you gonna find him?'

'I'm already workin' on it.'

'I suppose you're usin' your pals Jerry and Bardini?' he asked.

'Among others.'

Suddenly, Jack's face changed. He looked away from the two women and directly at me for the first time. Then he put his big hand on my shoulder and squeezed.

'You know, you really came through on this kidnappin' thing,' he said. 'Maybe it's time to think about givin' you a promotion.'

'To what?' I asked. 'I'm pretty happy with my job, Jack.' I was hoping he wasn't thinking about putting me in a position of more authority. I was pretty pleased with the amount of freedom my job gave me.

'Well,' he said, dropping his hand from my shoulder, 'it's just somethin' we can talk about later.'

'Sure,' I said, 'later.'

He turned his attention back to the women. I watched for a few moments, and of the five players at the table, they seemed to be the only ones who were winning consistently.

'I don't get it,' he said, shaking his head. 'But I will.'

As I walked away from Entratter I saw Jerry coming toward me. He'd changed his shirt and jacket, looked very casual with no tie.

'Hey, Mr G. What'd Mr Entratter want?'

'Just to be filled in. Apparently lawyer Rudin let Jack think he rescued me from the big bad police.'

'Mr Rudin ain't no criminal guy.'

'No, he's not,' I said, 'but if he wants to think he got me out, let 'im. I don't care. All I know is we have a small window that's closing by the minute.'

We'd spent most of the day driving around, hitting my contacts. We had about thirty-eight hours left.

'So now we just wait?'

'There's got to be more that we can do than wait,' I said.

'Like what?'

'Give me a minute.'

I figured we could go back to Irwin's studio and house and search again, but we'd been pretty thorough the last time.

'Irwin owns his house,' I said, 'but he doesn't own the studio. He rents it.'

'So?'

'So maybe we should talk to the landlord. Maybe even some of his neighbors. The stores on either side of him.'

'And ask 'em what?'

'I don't know,' I said. 'I'm wingin' it, Jerry. I just don't want to sit here and wait.'

'OK, then let's go.'

SIXTY-SIX

On the right of Irwin Studios was a T-shirt and gift shop. The grey-haired older lady behind the counter said, 'I just work here,' to everything we asked, and Jerry's size did nothing to intimidate her. Apparently, she'd seen enough in her life to know when to keep her mouth shut.

On the left side was a store that sold and fixed watches. The old guy behind the counter regarded us over the rims of thick glasses that had even thicker lenses, so he could do all the delicate work that was necessary with watches.

'Ain't seen Barney for a while,' he said to us. 'His place has been closed.'

'We know that,' I said. 'We were just wonderin' who the landlord was for this strip of stores, if it's even the same person.'

'It is,' the man said. 'Same landlord for this place, Irwin's, the T-shirt store and the one after that, the hardware store.'

'And who would that be?' I asked.

The grey-haired man looked at Jerry, who wasn't paying any attention to him. He was busy looking around at all the time pieces and clocks. There was a cuckoo clock on the wall that really seemed to attract his attention.

'That's a Black Forest Cuckoo,' he said to Jerry.

'Black Forest?'

'That's the area of Germany the wood comes from,' the man said. 'The Black Forest. That one was made by Hubert Herr in the nineteenth century.'

'Sir?' I said.

The man looked at me.

'The landlord?'

He took his glasses off, rubbed his eyes with his thumb and forefinger, then stared at me from beneath bushy grey eyebrows. 'That'd be me.'

'You're the landlord?'

'That's right. Been here thirty years.'

'My name is Eddie Gianelli,' I said. 'This is Jerry.'

'The name's Morheim,' the man said, 'Angus Morheim.'

'Mr Morheim, we're tryin' to find Barney Irwin.'

'You friends of his?'

His face was blank, revealing nothing about his feelings for Barney. But how many landlords really like their tenants?

I took a shot.

'Hell, no,' I said. 'Can't stand the guy.'

Now he made a face and said, 'That putz owes me two months rent. And when he leaves I'm gonna have to fumigate the place.'

'Is he leavin'?' I asked.

'He is if I don't get my rent.'

'Do you know where he lives?' I asked.

'I do, but he ain't been there either, for a while.'

'Would you know if he owns any other property? Or has a girlfriend he might be stayin' with?'

Morheim looked up at Jerry, who was still looking around at the merchandise.

'You gonna bust his head?' he asked.

'We might,' I said. 'That sorta depends on . . . a lot of things.'

'He ain't got a girlfriend I know of,' he said. 'Always chasin' skirts, though. Nice girl wouldn't have nothin' to do with him.'

'I see.'

'His friends ain't worth shit.'

'Do you know any of them?'

'No, but he hangs out at that bar around the corner.'

'Clipper's?'

'That's the one,' Morheim said. 'Buncha useless bastards in there.'

'Yeah, we've been there,' I said.

'That's it,' Morheim said. 'I don't know anywheres else he might be.'

'Well . . . OK,' I said. 'Thank you for talkin' to us.'

'When's it come out?' Jerry asked, suddenly.

'What?' Morheim asked.

Jerry pointed to the clock and asked, 'When's the bird come out?'

'On the hour,' Morheim said.

Still a half hour to go. I was hoping Jerry didn't want to stay and watch.

We started for the door and Morheim said, 'Wait a minute.'

'Yes?' I said, turning hopefully.

'Irwin's got a storage unit.'

And who says there's no hope?

'He does?'

'Yeah,' Morheim said, 'I know it because I got a unit in the same building. I seen him there a few times.'

'And where is that building?'

'Around the corner, down the street from the bar.'

'You wouldn't happen to know the unit number, would you?' I asked.

Morheim chose that moment to put his glasses back on. He looked down at the watch he'd had in his hand the whole time.

'Happens I do,' he said. 'Unit two twenty on the second floor.'

'Mr Morheim,' I said, 'thanks very much.'

'Do me a favor,' he said.

'What's that?'

'When you see that *Schweinhund*,' Morheim said, 'bust him one for me.'

'You got it, Mr Morheim,' Jerry said.

The old man looked up at Jerry and said, 'And you come back, I'll show you the clock.'

'I will,' Jerry said. 'Thanks.'

We stepped outside, letting the door close behind us.

'How do you do that?' I asked.

'What?'

'Get people to like you.'

'I'm a likeable guy, Mr G.,' he said. 'That's what makes me good at my job.'

'Hmm,' I said. 'Let's go check out that storage unit.'

SIXTY-SEVEN

We had parked around the corner, so we were able to walk to the storage facility, which was on the corner of the same block where Clipper's was. We walked past the bar while keeping to the other side of the street, then crossed over.

HI-POINT STORAGE the sign over the door said. I didn't know what it meant, but it didn't matter. You had to name your business something, right?

'We're gonna need your lock-picking skills again,' I said.

'Depends on the kind it is,' Jerry said. 'Places like this, people use all kinds of locks. If it's a combination lock we're fucked.'

'Well, let's find out.'

'How do we get up there?' Jerry asked.

'That'll be the easy part,' I said. 'You and me, we're lookin' for a unit that isn't on the first floor, but not too high up.'

'Like somethin' on the second floor?' Jerry asked.

'Exactly.'

We went inside.

Storage units were a new idea in the sixties. That meant they were built into existing buildings, not places specially designed for them. Those days were a long time coming.

This structure looked like it used to be an apartment building. The floors had been sectioned off into units of varying sizes and shapes. We went up the front stairs and through the double front doors.

The young man at the front desk gave us the whole sales pitch about how helpful it is to have a storage unit, how small businesses were able to increase their invoice, and not their overhead. We let him wind down and then told him we needed a unit off the main floor, but not too high up.

'Worried about fire?' he asked. 'We got sprinkler units on each floor, and plenty of fire escapes.'

'Still . . .' I said.

'Well, all right, then. We've got some available on the second floor,' he said. 'What size do you think you'll need?'

'What've you got?'

'Well, we've got some five by eights, some eight by tens, some ten by fifteens—'

'Why don't we start with an eight by ten?' I suggested.

'Fine. Do you need a lock? We have combination locks, or just key locks—'

'A lock and key will be good.'

I had to sign a one year contract and then he handed me a lock and key and said, 'If you'll wait a few minutes I can take you up, or you can just go on up yourself and have a look.'

'My partner and I will be OK on our own. We'll come back later with some stuff to store.'

'OK,' he said. 'Welcome to Hi-Point. Your unit is number two fifty-one.'

'Thanks.'

251 shouldn't be too far from 220, I thought. This was going well.

We took the elevator up one floor, got off and found 251 first, then walked down to 220. Irwin's unit was apparently one of the smaller five by eights. As we reached it we saw that things had suddenly stopped being easy.

'Damn!' I said.

We looked at each other, then at the door that had a combination lock.

'Look on the bright side, Mr G.,' Jerry said.

'What's that?'

'The lock is still there,' Jerry said. 'Maybe that means his stuff is still in there. Maybe he'll be back for it.'

'Well, we've got – what, thirty-five hours?' I said. 'I guess we could wait for him here, but then he might not show.'

'So? We can get in there.'

'How do we do that?'

'At night,' Jerry said.

'This place closes at five p.m.'

'Maybe I can't pick that lock,' he said, indicating the combo lock on the door, 'but did you notice the locks on this building? Easy.'

'OK, so we get into the building,' I said. 'How do we get into this unit?'

'The old-fashioned way,' he said.

SIXTY-EIGHT

We went back to the Sands briefly, to check if I'd gotten any calls. There were none.

'You put out so many feelers,' Jerry said, 'you'd think somebody woulda called by now.'

'Yeah,' I agreed. 'You'd think.'

We each changed into dark clothes, then drove to pick up some things Jerry said he'd need. After that we went back to the Hi-Point building and worked our way around to the back.

There was a collection of dumpsters, all full of garbage, lined up in the alley. The smell out there was something between rotten meat and piss.

Jerry whipped out his pen light and I held it for him while he worked the lock. He had also brought a small gym bag, which he laid near his feet.

'They think puttin' a metal door up is gonna keep people out,' he said, while he worked, 'but they forget that a lock is a lock.'

He continued to work while I looked up and down the alley, trying to hold the light still.

'Got it,' he finally said, and we were inside.

We found a back stairway and took it to the second floor. By the beam of his pen light we found the door of unit 220. He handed me the light again, put his bag down and took out a hammer.

'Why not a hacksaw?' I asked.

'That would take longer. But if this doesn't work I brought one.'

'What if there's a watchman downstairs?' I whispered.

'I'm gonna try and open it with one shot,' he said. 'If a watchman comes up I'll take care of him.'

'Don't kill him,' I said.

'Naw, Mr G.,' he said, 'don't worry. Just stand back.'

I backed away a few steps. Jerry brought the hammer back, then hit the lock with one solid whack . . . and it snapped open.

We both froze, waited to see if anyone would come up the steps looking to see what the noise was.

'I think we're OK,' I said.

He put the hammer away in the bag. The door was metal, on hinges. He removed the snapped lock, then slowly, quietly swung the door open.

SIXTY-NINE

There was a naked bulb hanging from the ceiling. I grabbed the short chain and yanked it, and the light came on.

File cabinets along one wall, the back, and down the other.

'Sonofabitch,' I said. 'I'll bet I know what's in these.'

He started at one end, me at the other, and all we found were nude photos of young girls.

'Goddamn,' I said, 'I wish I had a can of gasoline.'

'I know what ya mean.'

'Wait,' I said, closing the drawer of the cabinet I'd been looking through. I turned, went through another two cabinets until I found a drawer with 'D' names in them. Sure enough, I found what I was looking for.

'Sonofabitch!' I swore again. 'If Irwin was here right now I'd strangle him.' I was holding a whole sheaf of Abby Dalton photos.

'I guess I didn't scare him enough,' Jerry said, and he seemed genuinely disappointed with himself. 'I knew I shoulda broke somethin'.'

'Well, next time I'll hold him and you break his damn neck,' I said.

'So what do we do now?' Jerry asked. 'Wait for him to come back? Because he ain't gonna leave town without these photos. I'll bet he's got some other ones in there he wants as bad as those of Miss Dalton.'

'If we stake this place out it could take days, or weeks for him to show up,' I said. 'We don't have that much time.'

'What, then?'

I looked around.

'I suggest we go through the rest of these cabinets and see what we find,' I said. 'Maybe there's somethin' here that'll help us.'

'OK, Mr G.,' Jerry said. 'But . . .'

'What?' I said, detecting something in his tone.

'I just hope we don't find nothin' else that might make you wanna burn the whole buildin' down.'

I looked at the photos of Abby I was holding in my hands, and wondered what that would be.

As it turned out, the cabinets along the back wall – only three of them – held something quite different from the photos in all the others.

One cabinet had a drawer that was filled with financial reports, bills, tax records. The other two drawers were empty.

The second cabinet had one empty drawer, and two that seemed to be holding all sorts of personal records and papers that I really didn't want to go through. I already felt like I had to steam my hands clean when we got out of there.

The third cabinet was the emptiest. The top drawer was completely bare, the second held only one folder.

'What's that?' Jerry asked.

I took it out, opened it, knew exactly what it was right away.

'It's a floor plan,' I said.

'Of what?' Jerry asked.

'Harrah's, in Lake Tahoe.' That sonofabitch, I thought.

There was one more drawer to search, at the bottom. Jerry opened it while I was still staring at the floor plan, realizing the implications. It even included a drawing of the parking lots.

'Mr G.?'

'Yeah?'

'You better have a look.'

'What?'

I bent down and saw what he meant. There were some reels of film in the drawer. I took one out, and unfurled a length of it, holding it up to the light.

'Jesus,' I said, 'this opens up a whole new can of worms, Jerry.'

'Stag films?'

I nodded. We took another roll and had a look. Same thing. Men and women doing things to each other you should do at home, or in a hotel, or in a closet, but not on film.

'These look like good quality, Mr G.,' Jerry said. 'Maybe pro.'

'There's a lot more to Irwin than meets the eye, Jerry,' I said. I held a roll of film in one hand, and the Harrah's floor plan in the other. 'We been had, Jerry.' I waved the floor plan folder at him. 'Looks like Irwin was not only involved with the kidnapping. He may have planned the whole thing.'

SEVENTY

Barney Irwin was a kidnapper, and a producer of stag films. I wondered how many young girls who came to him for portraits ended up on film with their clothes off?

'What do we do?' Jerry asked.

'There's a lot of stuff here, Jerry,' I said. 'I doubt he'd want to leave it behind. In fact, I doubt that he's even leavin' town.'

'He ain't as scared, or as stupid, as we thought,' Jerry said.

'No, he's still stupid. Or else why leave this stuff lyin' around?'

'It ain't lyin' around,' Jerry said. 'It's under lock and key.'

'Still,' I said, 'this kidnap stuff, and the note I found in his desk drawer . . . not smart.'

'OK,' Jerry said, 'but he's tougher than we thought. He tried to have us both killed, tried to set us up again in that warehouse.'

'He's still in town,' I said. 'Maybe the Rienzas know where.'

'How do we find out?'

'We ask 'em.'

'I hope that don't mean goin' to a police station?' Jerry said.

'No,' I said, 'I'll just call Hargrove. Come on, let's lock up and get out of here.'

The combination lock wouldn't close again, but we managed to hang it on the door so it looked locked. Only Irwin, when he came to get inside, would know.

As we went down the back stairs I said, 'We're gonna need somebody to sit on this place and watch for Irwin to come back.'

'Not me.'

'No,' I said, 'I'll ask Danny to find somebody.'

We took the kidnap folder and a roll of film with us. I put them in the back seat while Jerry got behind the wheel.

'Where to?' he asked.

'Phone.'

'Pay phone?'

I thought a moment, then said, 'My house.'

'Is that smart? I mean, what if Irwin sends somebody after us again?'

'You'll take care of 'em.'

'As long as there's not more than three.'

When we walked into my house Jerry got a beer from the frig while I called Danny.

'Yeah, I got a guy who can sit on the place,' he said, after I told him everything we found. 'Stag films, huh? I hate those things. Most of the girls look strung out on somethin'.'

'For all we know Irwin's dealin' in drugs, too. The guy's real good at playin' dumb.'

'Well, maybe he's a pro when it comes to fuck films and drugs, but he's still an amateur when it comes to kidnapping.'

'Ain't that the truth. Listen, give your guy all my numbers and have him call as soon as he sees Irwin.'

'I'll have him tail him, and then call.'

'OK. Thanks, Danny.'

I hung up, called Hargrove at his office. He was there.

'You're running out of time, Eddie.'

'What about the Rienzas?' I asked. 'How are they doin' on time?'

'Better than you,' he said. 'They're out.'

'What?'

'Hit the streets hours ago.'

'How did that happen?'

'Their alibi checked out.'

'You said yourself about alibis—'

'Hey, if it checks out, it checks out,' he said. 'There's nothing I can do about it. I had to cut them loose.'

'That's great.'

'Watch your back,' Hargrove said. 'I think they were pretty mad at you.'

I hung up.

'So?' Jerry asked. 'They're out?'

'Yup.'

'Want a beer?'

'Yup.'

He tossed me a can. I caught it one handed.

'Now what?' he asked.

'I don't know, Jerry,' I said. 'We got the word out on Irwin, and we got his storage unit covered. I seriously don't know what else we can do. You got any suggestions?'

His eyes brightened and he said, 'Get somethin' to eat?'

SEVENTY-ONE

Morning came and we had twenty-four hours left to find Irwin and prove that he was responsible for Wayne's death. Also that he was involved in the kidnapping.

I took Jerry and the folder we had found to Jack Entratter's office at the Sands. We told him how we had come by it, and what we thought it meant.

'So,' Entratter said, 'it's not finished. Even if Irwin didn't plan the kidnapping, it's obvious he was involved and has to pay. Frank isn't gonna let anyone get off scot free.'

'He ain't gettin' off free,' Jerry said. 'Mr G. and me are gonna find him.'

'And we need to do it in the next twenty-four hours,' I said, 'or Jerry and I will be behind bars.'

'Well,' Entratter said, 'you ain't gonna find him sittin' here. Let me know if there's anythin' I can do to help.'

'Keep your lawyer on call, Jack,' I said. 'He may have to get us outta jail.'

'You got it.'

We left Entratter's office, took the elevator down to the hotel lobby, where I stopped dead.

'What is it, Mr G.?'

I stared at him for a moment, then said, 'I don't know where to go next, Jerry.'

'We could go sit on his storage unit,' Jerry said.

'Danny's already got a guy on it,' I said. 'What's the point of the three of us there?'

'So is there any place else we can look?'

'I figured with all the stops we made we would have gotten a call by now,' I said. 'We've got less than a day.'

'You really think Hargrove would be that much of a dick?'

'Oh yeah,' I said, 'I do.'

'Maybe we should do some more drivin' around, then,' Jerry said.

A bellman came walking over.

'Mr Gianelli, hotel operator's got a call for you. They won't hang up until we find you.'

'OK, thanks,' I said. 'I'll get it on a house phone.'

'Yes, sir.'

I took Jerry over to a bank of phones and picked one up.

'Operator, it's Eddie Gianelli. You have a call for me?'

'Yes, sir, I'll put it through.'

I waited only a few seconds and then a girl said, 'Eddie? It's Darla.'

'Hey, Darla,' I said, raising my eyebrows at Jerry. 'We were just talkin' about you.'

'Good things I hope, love,' she said.

'Only the best. You got somethin' for me?'

'I've got a location where your guy might be hidin' out,' she said.

'Where'd you get this info?'

'I put the word out on the street, same as you. One of my people got back to me.'

'OK,' I said. 'So where is this place?'

'Out in the desert.'

'The desert's a big place, hon.'

'Well,' she said, 'the exact location is gonna cost ya, Eddie.'

'You'll get paid, Darla,' I said. 'You know you can trust me.'

'We just have to agree on a price, Eddie,' she said. 'Then I'll trust you for it.'

'How about two hundred?' I asked.

'How about two thousand?' she asked. 'Is this important to ya?'

Important enough that I didn't really want to haggle, but I was probably going to have to do business with her in the future.

'Five hundred, Darla.'

'A thousand and you got a deal.'

'OK,' I said. 'A grand. Now give.'

'He's at the Sunshine Ranch.'

'That's just outside of Indian Springs, right?'

'That's the one.'

One of the things the casinos had to supply for their clients was women, which meant we had to know where the women were. And if they weren't on the street, they were in the ranches out in the desert. Many had been closed down as public nuisances in 1951, but the ones that continued to operate had a 'special' relationship with the law.

'Darla, is he there now?'

'I been hangin' on the phone for you a while, Eddie,' she said, 'but when I made the call, he was still there. That's why I wouldn't hang up till I talked to ya.'

'And you're positive this is a place he goes?'

'He goes there a lot, Eddie,' she said. 'He owns it.'

Well, maybe that explained where Irwin got some of his girls for his stag films.

'Baby, if he's there you earned every penny,' I assured her.

'I'll be waitin', lover.'

I hung up.

'What's near Indian Springs?' Jerry asked.

'The Sunshine Ranch,' I said. 'It's a brothel. A cathouse.'

'Whores?'

'Lots of 'em.'

'And that's where Irwin is?'

'He was when she made the call.'

'How far away is that?' he asked.

'Maybe an hour.'

We stood there and stared at each other for a few moments. The same thing was going through our heads. Call Hargrove and walk away, or drive out there and get Irwin ourselves?

'Let's do it,' Jerry said, and I nodded.

SEVENTY-TWO

For a long time I'd been of the opinion that prostitution in Las Vegas should be legalized. Not so much the street trade, like Darla, but the girls who worked the hotels and ranches out in the desert. Once that was done, Las Vegas would become the place people could go to get *anything* they wanted.

We kicked up a lot of dust as most of the drive was on dirt roads. Eventually, we came within sight of a structure and I put my hand on Jerry's arm. He braked and let the car idle.

'That it?' he asked.

'Should be.'

'Don't look like much.'

'Some of them actually look like a ranch,' I said, 'but this one . . .'

This one looked like a worn out double-wide. There were a couple of cars parked out front.

'Let's back up some, just till we're out of sight,' I said. 'Then we'll walk the rest of the way.'

He put the Caddy in reverse. We only had to go about twenty yards. I directed Jerry to pull off the road. If anyone came along maybe they'd think we'd gotten stuck and had to walk.

We got out of the car and, since we were in the desert, left our jackets in the car. I could see Jerry's .45 tucked into the back of his pants.

Once we started out on foot I looked around, imagining that this was the same view a cowboy would've seen a hundred years ago when he was out here on a horse. That is, until we once again came within view of the trailer.

'Let's circle and come in from the back,' I suggested.

'Good idea.'

From that angle we could see how large the structure actually was. An extension had been built on the back, which probably housed rooms – or cribs – for the girls.

We couldn't walk right in and pretend to be customers. Irwin had seen both of us, would know us on the spot. Of course, we could've taken the chance that he wouldn't notice us till too late, but with girls and customers around some innocent people could have gotten hurt if there was gun play.

And there were customers. We saw a few cars parked alongside the trailer's extension. And there were those two out front. Some of the cars must have belonged to employees, so I was hoping the interior wasn't going to be too crowded.

There was a back door at the very end of the extension, but if we went in that way we'd probably have to bypass every room in the place.

'There's gotta be another door, maybe on the other side,' Jerry said.

We circled completely around the building and, sure enough, found a side door about halfway up the extension. There were also three motorcycles parked there. Not only was Irwin probably inside, but the Rienzas, as well.

We'd done this before, even though neither of us was an expert at breaking and entering. There were windows on either side of the door. The window on the right was blocked with something, so it was probably a crib. The window to the left was clear, and the room appeared to be an office. We saw a desk, a lamp, and a sofa. We could only see half the sofa, though, so we saw half a man lying on it – the bottom half. However, that half was clad in lime green pants, and white shoes.

'That's him,' I whispered.

'Gotta be,' Jerry said.

Instead of having the bad luck to have to use the back door, we ran into good luck. Once we got through this side door we'd be right next to the room Barney Irwin was in.

Jerry dropped to one knee and started working with his lock picks. I kept looking both ways – actually, all ways; left, right, behind us and above. I was sweating, and it wasn't just from the sun beating down on us. The back of Jerry's shirt was soaked through, but knowing him that *was* from the sun.

Irwin might still be dressing like a buffoon, but we'd discovered he was more than that. This might not be as easy as we'd hoped. It wasn't necessarily just girls, customers, other employees and Irwin inside. He could have a couple of mugs with him.

I heard the lock go *snick* and patted Jerry on his damp shoulder. He was getting better at that.

He stood up, looked at me and indicated he would take the lead. I nodded. He slid his .45 from his belt, held it in his right hand, and put his left hand on the door knob.

He looked at me. Again, I nodded, and he opened the door.

SEVENTY-THREE

We stepped inside, closing the door behind us. Irwin may not have spent much money on the worn outer shell of the place, but the inside was air-conditioned. My soaked shirt immediately felt like a coat of ice on me.

We moved down a short hall, which led to a longer one that ran the center of the extension. Jerry peered out to be sure we were clear, then waved me on with his left hand as he stepped out. At any minute a girl and her john could come walking up or down the hall. We quickly moved to the door of the office. Jerry grabbed the knob, turned it and the door opened. We sprang into the room; I pulled the door closed behind, quickly, without slamming it.

'What the hell is it now?' Irwin demanded from the sofa. 'Can't a guy catch a nap—'

He stopped when Jerry put the barrel of his .45 to Irwin's cheek.

'What the fuck?' Irwin said.

I moved around so he could see me. When he did, he craned his head against the pressure of the .45 and saw Jerry.

'Fuck me,' he said.

'That's exactly what we're here to do, Barney,' I said.

'Hey, guys, look,' Irwin said, 'there's no hard feelins—'

'Cut the crap, Barney,' I said. 'You tried to have us killed, and we saw what's in your storage unit. So cut the crap.'

Irwin looked at me and asked, 'Can I sit up?'

'Let him up, Jerry.'

Jerry moved the barrel of the gun far enough to let Irwin upright.

'You guys are in trouble,' Irwin said, his entire attitude doing a one-eighty. 'You don't think I'm here without back-up, do you?'

'We don't care,' Jerry said, 'We seen the kinda help you hire.'

Irwin looked at Jerry, then surprised me by smiling.

'You're right, of course,' he said. 'Maybe you'd consider coming to work for me?'

'Sorry,' Jerry said, 'I don't work for guys who wear white shoes.'

Irwin looked down at his feet, still smiling.

'Barney,' I said, 'you know who Jerry is and what he does, right?'

'Oh yeah,' Irwin said, 'I checked him out after that day in the warehouse.'

'Then you know he'd kill you.'

'Yes.'

'Then get up,' I said. 'We're walkin' out of here. And if you make a ruckus, Jerry's gonna pull the trigger of that forty-five. It might even blow your head completely off your shoulders.'

'I doubt that, Eddie,' Irwin said, 'but I'm sure it would blow the top of my head off, so I get your point.'

He stood up. Now that he wasn't playing the lecherous photographer he even stood differently.

'Where we goin'?' he asked.

'I'm gonna deliver you to a detective named Hargrove,' I said. 'With the Las Vegas PD.'

'You can't prove anything.'

'That's his job,' I said. 'He's gonna prove that you either killed Wayne or had him killed. I'm sure he'll get one or both of the Rienza brothers to admit you hired them to kill me. He won't be able to prove you sent three hoods to Brooklyn to kill Jerry. But he will be able to prove that you were involved in the kidnapping of Frank Sinatra Jr. In fact, he might even prove you planned the whole thing.'

'What?' He'd still been grinning until I mentioned the kidnapping. 'What the hell? That was my brother's thing, not mine.'

'We found the floor plan of Harrah's in your storage unit, Barney,' I said. 'And a note in your desk drawer. Silly of you to keep those things.'

'None of it,' Irwin said. 'You can't prove any of it.'

'I only told him I'd deliver you,' I said. 'Proving anythin' is his job. Let's go.'

'You heard him,' Jerry said.

'The Rienzas are here, you know,' Irwin said. 'With a couple of the girls.'

'Let's hope they stay busy,' I said. 'For their benefit as much as yours.'

Irwin patted his pockets, as if he'd forgotten something, then looked around.

'You won't need a jacket,' I said. 'Let's go, out the side door.'

He nodded, and headed for the door. Jerry put his hand out to stop him, went to the door first. He looked out, then waved us to follow. He kept his gun in his hand.

We could hear girls laughing and men moaning, but we made it out the side door without running into anyone. We headed to the front of the building, intending to walk him to my car. But as we passed the front door it opened and a Rienza brother stepped out.

'Hey, boss, where you goin'—' he started to shout, but then he saw Jerry.

'Get 'em!' Irwin shouted, and dropped to the ground.

The other Rienza came through the door and they both pulled their guns.

'Jerry, get down!' I yelled, but he had a gun and I didn't. Jerry knocked me down, then turned to face the Rienzas in what seemed like an Old West gunfight.

SEVENTY-FOUR

The anniversary party was in full swing in the Sands Ballroom when we got there. We'd taken the time to shower the desert off us, treat our cuts and bruises, and then dress for the party.

There was a band playing, and people dancing. Waitresses dressed like showgirls – or maybe they were showgirls – were working the room, carrying trays of hors d'oeuvre and drinks. Celebrities were also working the room, mixing with the guests. I spotted Dino and Joey, Jack Jones, Nat King Cole, Steve and Eydie, Tony Bennett, Richard Conte . . . they had all turned out for the Sands' eleventh anniversary.

We found Jack Entratter standing with a group of people, including Jilly Rizzo, Frank, and the Mayor of Las Vegas.

The Mayor was rambling on – as he was prone to do – which meant that Jack was scanning the room. He spotted us approaching.

'What the hell happened to you?' he asked.

I touched the band-aid above my left eye.

'Oh, Jerry knocked me down.'

'What?'

'That's OK,' I said. 'It was just to save my sorry ass.'

'Wait a minute,' Entratter said. He interrupted the Mayor just long enough to excuse himself, then grabbed my sore left arm and pulled me to the side. Jerry followed along, snagging a pig-in-a-blanket from a passing girl.

'OK,' he said, 'now tell me what the hell happened with you two?'

I explained to him about finding out where Irwin was, and driving out there to get him. How we grabbed him, but Jerry had to shoot it out with the Rienza brothers while we were getting away.

'Oh, Christ. Are they dead?' he asked.

'Oh, yeah,' Jerry said.

'Jesus . . .'

'Jerry pushed me out of the way, then turned on them – it was like somethin' outta the Wild West, Jack. Guns blazin', and those boys hittin' the ground.'

Entratter looked at Jerry.

'And you?'

'A few scratches,' he said. 'I lost my footin' and fell down.'

'And then you just left?'

'Naw,' I said, 'once the shootin' was over we called the Sheriff's Department, and when they came out we had them call the Las Vegas PD. They cuffed us all, but when Hargrove got there they let us go.'

'Hargrove let you go?'

'Hey, we gave him Irwin for murder, and kidnappin'. Believe me, he's real happy.'

'He's gotta prove it all.'

'I'm thinkin' the other kidnappers won't wanna take the rap without good ol' Barney,' I told him. 'I don't know about the murder, but that should put him away for a good long time. Besides, we also found out he's been producing illegal porn. Believe me, he ain't goin' nowhere for a while.'

'So you're off the hook for murder?'

'Looks like.'

'And they ain't gonna go after Jerry for killin' the Rienza boys?'

I shook my head.

'Self-defense.'

'What about his gun?'

'They took it away from me,' Jerry muttered, mournfully.

'And they ain't gonna charge you?'

'Hargrove said he'd see what he could do about that,' I said.

'Don't worry. I ain't gonna sweat a gun charge, Mr Entratter.'

'You'll have one of our lawyers, Jerry,' Jack assured him. 'So you won't have to.'

'Thanks, Mr E.,' Jerry said. 'Is there food here? I mean, other than this small stuff?'

'There's a buffet table on the other side of the room.'

Jerry took off.

'Maybe I shouldn't have told him that,' Jack said, watching big Jerry bull his way to the other side of the room.

'He would've found it, anyway.'

'Come on, Eddie,' Jack said, slapping me on the shoulder, 'let's get you a drink, and then you can tell Frank that the last motherfucker who kidnapped his kid is in custody.'

EPILOGUE

December 12, 2006

It was Frank's birthday.

The Chairman of the Board passed in 1998, but every year on his birthday I still missed him.

At my age I don't drive so good anymore, so when I want to go out at night I get myself a driver. That's why I was in the back seat of the car, on my way to celebrate Frank's birthday.

After all the kidnappers were caught they began to turn on one another. Convicting them was no problem. Oddly, the Irwins disappeared. I never did hear what had happened to them. Keenan and Amsler – friends since childhood – served just under five years each. When they got out they walked the straight and narrow. I'd seen Amsler's obit earlier in the year, in May. He died at 65 of liver failure.

All but about six thousand dollars of the money was recovered. One of the kidnappers – Amsler or Keenan, I don't remember – had bought his mother a bunch of new furniture. When Frank heard that the law was getting ready to repossess it, he told them to let the woman keep her furniture.

Reading Amsler's obit had made me remember when Frank saw Amsler at the Liston-Patterson fight earlier in sixty-three. I wondered if that's when the kidnappers had started to hatch their plot, and were in Vegas to see Irwin??

Frank was so pleased with what all the cops and FBI agents did that he gave them each a two-thousand-dollar gold watch made from twenty-dollar gold pieces, with velvet hands. There were twenty-seven of them.

The FBI returned the watches to Frank with a letter from Dean Elson, Special Agent in charge of the Las Vegas office. He told Frank that FBI agents were not permitted to accept gifts. A few weeks later Frank bought another one and sent it to J. Edgar Hoover, himself. He also sent the other watches along with it for each of the agents, with thanks for all the FBI had done to recover his son.

This time, they were not returned. Frank had always felt he'd made a mistake the first time by not including a watch for J. Edgar.

He tried to give me a watch, as well, but I didn't take it. I had done it all out of friendship. And I was a little miffed that he sent me the same thing he sent all those others. After all, I thought we were friends. But I called Frank to thank him, asked him not to take offense. He said there had to be something he could do for me. I explained about Jerry and his cousin Billy, and Frank stopped me before I was done. A couple of days later Jerry called me after he heard from the Sands that the debt was forgiven.

'How did you do that, Mr G.?' he asked.

'How do you know I did it?' I asked. 'Maybe Frank did it.'

'I'll bet the call came from Mr S., but I'll bet even more that it was your idea.'

'Don't be like the FBI and look a gift horse in the mouth, Jerry. What's done is done.'

'Well, thanks, Mr G.'

'You gonna tell Billy he's off the hook?'

'Naw,' Jerry said, 'he's makin' payments to me, figurin' I'll send it to the casino. I'll let him keep doin' that, and eventually I'll give him the money back. You know, like one of them Christmas Clubs in the bank.'

'You're a hard man, Jerry.'

'Not you, Mr G.,' Jerry said. 'You're just a softy . . .'

The kidnappers tried a pretty wild defense. They claimed the whole kidnapping was bogus, planned by Frank Jr. himself for publicity. The Independent News Service in London latched on to the story and ran with it. Frank sued them and won a boatload of money, which he then donated to charity. He just wanted to keep the record clean.

The limo pulled up in front of the restaurant where I was to have dinner. It was off the strip, a local place my dinner partner and I picked out because celebrities didn't go there.

As the driver got out to open my door I thought back to the premiere of *Robin and The 7 Hoods*. After the trial Frank went back to work and the guys finished the film. It was released the following year. It wasn't a great movie, but it had been fun, a good distraction for Frank from the whole JFK fiasco. After Frankie was snatched it was kind of a chore to go back to. I always enjoyed watching the film, though, just not as much as I enjoyed *Ocean's 11.*

The cast members were pretty much all gone. Tony Randall died a couple of years ago. Peter Falk was still around, but I never did meet him. I know Barbara Rush – who played Marian in the film – and she had once told me what a difficult shoot that was for Frank.

The driver opened my door and said, 'We're here, Mr G.'

'Thanks, Carl.'

He gave me a hand getting out of the back seat, and then walked inside with me. He'd sit in a corner and have a meal on me, so that I wouldn't have to wait for him to pick me up after.

I walked into the dining room of the restaurant, crossed the floor to the table where my dinner partner was seated. As I approached he stood up, smiled broadly, and stuck out his hand. Damned if he didn't remind me of his dad.

'Hiya, Frankie.'

BIBLIOGRAPHY

Rat Pack Confidential by Shawn Levy, Doubleday, 1998; *The Rat Pack* by Lawrence J. Quirk and William Schoell, Perennial, 1998; *Dino* by Nick Tosches, Dell Publishing, 1992; *His Way, The Unauthorized Biography of Frank Sinatra* by Kitty Kelley, Bantam Books, 1986; *The Peter Lawford Story, Life With The Kennedys, Monroe and The Rat Pack* by Patricia Seaton Lawford, Carroll & Graf Publishers, 1988; *Mouse in The Rat Pack, The Joey Bishop Story* by Michael Seth Starr, Taylor Trade Publishing, 2002; *The Frank Sinatra Film Guide* by Daniel O'Brien, BT Batsford, 1998; *Casino, Love and Honor in Las Vegas* by Nicholas Pileggi, Simon & Schuster, 1995; *Las Vegas is My Beat* by Ralph Pearl, Bantam Books, 1973, 1974; *Murder in Sin City, The Death of a Las Vegas Casino Boss* by Jeff German, Avon Books, 2001; *A Short History of Reno*, by Barbara and Myrick Land, University of Nevada Press, 1995; *A Short History of Las Vegas* by Barbara and Myrick Land, University of Nevada press, 1999, 2004; *When The Mob Ran Vegas* by Steve Fischer, Berkline Press, 2005, 2006; *My Life With Frank Sinatra* by George Jacobs and William Stadiem, HarperCollins, 2003).